Red August

Peggy Estes

Girl in the Middle Publishing, July 2016

ISBN: 978-0-9977223-0-7

Special thanks to:

David Shenberger of IDCreative,
for the beautiful book jacket.

Prologue

I was born on the first day of August — the month of searing yellow heat and sparkling green jewels, and it was during that month of summer climax at a turning point in my life that I found myself at the center of an intrigue, both terrifying and exhilarating.

The sparkling green jewels are the August birthstone — peridot. My mother frequently gave me that light green jewelry for my birthday. Looking back with the advantage of all that I know now, perhaps there was a desperate purpose to that ritual. She may have regretted her choices where I was concerned and was trying to create a different reality. My mother tended to sugarcoat the truth or avoid it altogether. That was her coping mechanism as a socially disadvantaged woman stuck in a troubled marriage with very few resources.

So, when the trauma occurred in our family, we had devastating consequences to deal with, but no one really talked about it. My sister's search for a confidante took a tragic turn. My quest for the truth turned me into a writer. From an early age, something deep in my spirit whispered to me that there were dark secrets in our house and liberating truths to uncover. In retrospect, it remains to be seen if the truth was worth unleashing the dark.

In any case, I have always associated August with the smell of wild honeysuckle, the incessant buzz of cicadas, and that light green peridot color. Until the August that opened forbidden doors that changed everything, including the way I perceive simple old adages, because it really all began with a disturbing dream, and a walk in the park.

> Ruby January
> Mississippi River Bluffs
> Late August

Chapter 1

There was a thunderstorm brewing across the river in St. Louis and I ignored the speed limit and opened up the Jag as I drove to La Vista Park. It was a nice respite from the summer heat and my dog, Jonah, hung out of the back passenger window, excited at the prospect of a run. I opened my window as well, enjoying the cool, natural air from the oncoming storm as I drove onto the parking lot.

La Vista Park has a paved path that cuts through prairie grass and then winds down through the bluffs, where it follows a creek to the Great River Road. I pulled my knife sheath out of the console, clipped it to my belt and strapped it down on my jeans-clad thigh. Then I opened the door for Jonah and let him race ahead, carrying his lead with me in case I needed it. I don't always wear my dagger when I'm hiking a trail, but this particular path gets very secluded on the lower wooded section, and I had learned the hard way that there are men in this world with wrong intentions. I had lost that innocent belief we have in our youth that bad things only happen to other people.

Off to the right, a woman was harvesting the last of the season's tomatoes in the Discovery Garden. The garden is a shared community site where local growers occasionally give educational seminars.

The wind was picking up and a pretty little dark-haired girl of about five was laughing at her brother's attempts to fly a bright yellow kite. She suddenly noticed Jonah and ran captivated alongside him.

"Look at that doggie! He's beautiful!"

Jonah obliged by giving her a playful pounce forward, and then went streaking away, hoping she would give chase. I followed him with my normal assertive pace, as I soaked in the vibrant nature around me.

On the lower portion, I stopped to lean against a wooden fence and watch Jonah splash around in the creek below. The sun pierced through the trees in shards as it retreated from the advancing storm and I closed my eyes, enjoying the warmth on my face, and thought about the recurring dream that had awakened me abruptly in the early morning hours.

The dream was of a house on the bluffs of Grafton — a house that appeared perfectly respectable, except for the dark whisper calling to me from its depths. That whisper was a remnant from my girlhood — something I had buried in a far corner of my memory, but which now seemed intent on resurfacing and making its presence known. I had no connection to that house and no knowledge regarding it, but it drew me with a seductive force that made me afraid to enter it in the dream and left me feeling unsettled when I awoke.

Jonah darted up the creek bank, shaking off the excess water and drawing me from my uneasy speculation. We headed back up the hill. The hill is what keeps the physically unfit out of La Vista Park. It's a very steep quarter-mile trek back up to the prairie.

I had just reached the top when I saw Jonah glance back at me uncertainly, and then break into a run. Then I saw the huge Rottweiler come charging out of the woods after him. La Vista is a popular spot for dog walkers, but it isn't normal to see one unaccompanied.

I felt a surge of fear for Jonah that quickly gave way to anger that this was happening after all my careful work to bring him out of his shell, and I broke into a hard run as the Rott caught up to him and knocked him to the ground. I wondered how a Rottweiler had managed to catch up to Jonah. I had seen Jonah come dangerously close to catching squirrels, he was so fast.

By the time I got to them he had Jonah by the neck, growling and thrashing him. I launched myself into the air and delivered a solid kick to the Rottweiler's ribs. He yelped in surprise and went rolling across the grass as I fell back onto the path - the thunk of flesh against pavement jarring me for an instant. He turned towards me with a snarl as I got back on my feet, pulled my dagger out and looked him in the eye.

"Now you get!" I commanded and waved the knife towards the woods. He stood his ground, growling at me and weighing his chances. "Go on! Get!" I continued to yell at him.

I didn't want to stab him. I didn't want to hurt any animal, but I would if I had to. He seemed to be wavering, so I took a threatening step forward, pulling the dagger back into strike position. He suddenly relented and ran back to the woods.

I slipped the knife back into the sheath and went to check on Jonah. Luckily, his skin wasn't broken, but he was still shaking. I squatted down to soothe him, wrapping my arms around him and whispering that it was okay, and he tentatively thumped his tail for me.

"I've always heard you shouldn't look an aggressive dog in the eye, but it seemed to work out okay for you."

I looked up to see a stunning blonde woman in matching blue Nike shorts and tee walking towards us on the path.

"He's a beautiful dog," she said and reached to pet him.

Jonah recoiled from her and ran ahead towards the car.

"He's just shaken up right now," I told her as I got to my feet, keeping an eye on him.

"That's okay. I would be too if I'd just been attacked."

There was something peculiar in the tone of her voice and I turned back for a closer look. Long blonde hair that was strategically highlighted, eyes a color somewhere between blue and green, good skin, perfect bone structure, and a figure made faultless by Pilates or some other designer workout regimen - the type of visual presentation that induces men to make fools of themselves and puts lesser women immediately on guard. She glanced down at my sheath.

"It's not typical to see a woman run off a Rottweiler...or wear a knife strapped to her thigh." Her look was challenging.

"I'm not a typical woman."

She gave a short laugh. "Neither am I." She held out her hand. "Angelique Vaughn."

I drew a surprised breath, caught off-guard as I had heard that name from someone significant, then accepted her hand. Her grip was firm, and I gave her a few points for that. I hate a limp handshake.

"Ruby January."

She glanced back towards the spot where Jonah had disappeared into tall grass.

"He looks part German shepherd. It's very odd that he ran from a fight. He might have taken that Rott if he hadn't run."

She turned back to me and held my eyes for a long moment. Jonah is a fairly good size, and he does have some of the coloring and markings of a German shepherd, but as a puppy he had been terrorized by a Rottweiler at the farmhouse where he was born. He had eventually been rescued by a neighbor and taken to a shelter, from which I had adopted him. I was tempted to defend Jonah, but my instincts told me not to share.

"It's important to know who you are, Ruby," she finally said. "It can mean the difference between life and death."

Before I could respond, she turned and jogged away. I watched her for a moment, then turned and sprinted ahead. Jonah came out of the field and fell into step with me on the path. He seemed to be recovering nicely, secure in the strong bond I had patiently built with him.

As we passed the Discovery Garden, I noticed the woman had pulled the little girl inside and was watching me suspiciously. I was used to that. Not many women openly carry a weapon and other women often looked askance at me. The boy, however, had climbed up on the fence and he gave me a big grin.

"That was *sick* how you chased that dog away!"

I flashed him a smile, then turned and glanced back down the trail. Angelique was poised at the top of the hill, watching us. She waved suddenly, then turned and jogged out of sight.

*****

Chapter 2

The River Road, with its rugged beauty, is in my blood. No matter where I travel or whatever wonders I see, I know my place on this earth. I have always lived near it and key events in my life were connected to it. The Great River Road is actually a route along the river through several states, but the section I grew up on runs along the Illinois border of St. Louis, Missouri, spanning four lanes across and 14 miles long. It begins in the scenic town of Grafton, Illinois, where I spent my childhood, runs past the confluence of the Illinois River with the mighty Mississippi and down to the historic city of La Vista. Stone Ledge, where I live now, is a small, private cluster of upscale homes set in the bluffs, halfway between the two.

The river was devoid of boats, due to the impending storm, and hawks were circling lazily over bluffs dotted with green summer foliage as the mysterious house drew me inexorably west. A Harley roared by in the passing lane, evoking memories of riding this road on the back of Chase January's bike. I had loved that sense of adventure, the feel of my arms wrapped around his waist, the sun glinting off the water, the wind in my hair, and the powerful bike vibrating under our thighs. I was never a biker chick, per se, but Chase is a man's man and riding a Harley was part of his appeal.

I glanced back at Jonah in his position at the window. He looked happy to be riding along. I envy dogs their ability to set aside painful experiences and live in the moment. It took me years to learn that lesson.

I slowed down as I approached Grafton, the speed limit greatly reduced so the tourists could cruise through town at a leisurely pace. When I was growing up it was just a quiet little river town with a grade school, a few churches and some businesses, but also its share of bars and street-tough types. I first learned to protect myself in the back alleys of Grafton.

After the 'Great Flood of '93,' half of the houses had been demolished on the order of the Federal Emergency Management Agency (FEMA), and you could not rebuild in the flood plain. People were given generous buyouts and their property was absorbed for green space or parking lots. The residential population was reduced by half, but in their place, on higher ground, arose wineries, antique shops, bed and breakfasts, and trendy pubs, along with the new Grafton Marina, giving the area a quaint tourist feel.

The town is now a popular destination for summer boating, fall color touring, and weekend drinking. People also stop on their way up to Pere Marquette State Park, just a few miles northwest of town and my stomping grounds when I was in high school.

I drove resolutely up Main Street until I reached the parking lot of St. Patrick's Catholic Church – the small parish I was raised in, its yellow stone façade still solid, steeple rising towards the source of my interest. I got out and leaned back against the Jag, taking in the house on the bluff. It hadn't been there when I was a child, and I wasn't sure exactly when it had been erected, as I don't venture back to Grafton that often – at least, not that far into town. It was comprised of stone and featured two multi-story windows that promised a spectacular view. It sat imperiously above the more modest houses below, as if it were holding court.

The breeze from the approaching storm was playfully lifting my hair. I glanced around to ensure I was alone, then swayed forward, raising my face to the house and closing my eyes. I lifted my arms, palms open and slowed my breathing until I was in a relaxed, self-hypnotic state. I suggested the dream to my mind, picturing myself once again standing in front of the house. The dark whisper called to me from within and the pull I felt was a paradox - at once welcoming and forbidding. I wrestled with it momentarily, but finally resisted its disturbing lure and turned to start down a path that cuts through the bluffs. I knew what lay ahead.

"Ruby!" I came back to reality with a start. "Are you all right?"

I vaguely recognized the striking middle-aged woman, though I hadn't seen her in many years. I tried to recall her name. It was something like mine, but even less common...Jewel. Jewel Alexander. I had occasionally seen her at Mass when I was a teenager.

"Yes, I'm fine." I gave her an embarrassed laugh, knowing how that must have looked. "You're Jewel, right?"

She nodded. "I just stopped by to see the church. I just got back into town and haven't been inside in years. It's still as pretty as ever."

"Yes, it's a pretty little church," I agreed.

She looked up at the house for a moment, then turned back to me, curiosity in her brown eyes. Shiny, dark blonde hair still fell below her shoulders in a flattering side part that I had always thought made her look like the noir era movie star, Veronica Lake. Her figure still looked lean and strong under olive green cargo pants and a black, scoop-neck tee.

"You seem very interested in that house." Her voice was low and rich. "Do you know who lives there?"

"No. Do you?"

She shook her head and watched me silently for a moment, but her expression gave away nothing.

"Who's your friend?" she suddenly asked, nodding towards the car. She was already walking towards Jonah with her hand out and he climbed halfway out the window to meet her. She stroked his face and seemed to be looking deeply into his eyes.

"That's Jonah," I told her. "He doesn't usually warm up to strangers that quickly."

"I've always had a way with animals," she responded.

"Me too," I said with a smile.

"He's been traumatized." It was more statement than question.

"Yes," I said, somewhat taken aback, then surprised myself by sharing, "He was attacked by a Rottweiler when he was a puppy." I hesitated for a moment, then added, "And again less than an hour ago on a hiking trail."

She looked back at me sharply. "What happened?"

I told her, briefly, and she turned back to Jonah, stroking his ears, and leaned down to whisper something to him that I couldn't hear. He licked her face.

"I was just about to take a walk through town. Would you and Jonah like to join me?" She turned to me with an engaging smile.

"Okay."

I hadn't walked through Grafton in years, but I wasn't ready to part from her yet. I felt strangely drawn to her. I reached under the seat for Jonah's lead and clipped it on his collar, locked the car and followed her out to the sidewalk. She headed east, towards the River Road. We walked in companionable silence for a couple of minutes, taking in the scenery. I sneaked a glance at her.

"Do you live here in town?" I asked.

"I've been traveling for several years, and I've just come back for a visit."

"Where have you been?"

"Europe, mostly – Italy and England. I was in Egypt for a while, in Cairo, until the political situation turned ugly."

I wondered what she did for money and how she was able to travel. I didn't recall her having a career.

"Have you ever been married?" I ventured.

She shook her head. "No, I never have. But you have, I take it?"

"Yes. To Chase January. We're divorced now."

"But you kept his name? You're not going by Winslow anymore."

"It didn't feel right to go back to that name. I'm not that girl anymore. I kept my son's name – my only child. He's away at college."

She thought about that for a moment. "You must have had him right out of high school."

"Yes, actually. I never thought I'd be one of those girls who got married right out of high school, but that's what happened. Chase was several years older than me. He was a good-looking guy and he had a personality that was hard to resist, but he was also very dependable, and I needed someone dependable back then." I didn't elaborate and she didn't probe, which I appreciated. "Were you born around here?" I asked her.

"No, I was born in Europe, on an American military base. My father was an officer in the Air Force and we moved around a lot. The traveling is in my blood. I get restless staying in one place for too long."

"What brought you to this area? Scott Air Force Base?"

"No. The age-old female dilemma. I followed a man here." She stopped walking and turned towards the river, an indecipherable look on her face. "Even after he left, I stayed on for a while. There's a charm about this place. I felt drawn to come back and see it again." She smiled at me. "And you? You no longer live here in town, right?"

I shook my head. She pointed behind me, and I turned to see my old family property. I'd been so engrossed, I hadn't noticed where we were walking. For a moment, I was lost in old emotions.

"I guess they demolished it after the Great Flood?" she asked.

"Yes."

All that remained were the tiger lily patch my mother had planted, blooming now in late summer, and the big elm tree in the back yard. The foundation for the house had been filled in and planted over with grass seed.

"I heard that your mother died in a car accident," she said.

"Yes, with my stepdad. It's unclear what caused him to run off the road. My real father died a few years before that." I didn't want to talk about him, so I wandered towards the elm tree.

"What became of your sister?" she asked.

"Rachael is gone too. She died in a fall from the bluffs not long after my mother's death."

"What caused her fall?"

I looked her squarely in the eye. "I'm not sure."

She nodded but said nothing.

I turned to look at the elm tree. The wind was whipping its branches around, evoking nostalgic memories in me. There was something about the woman that made me trust her, and I don't trust anyone easily.

"When I was a little girl," I told her, "I would dance in the wind that precedes a thunderstorm." I walked over to the elm, held out my arms and felt the wind racing through my fingers. "It would come rushing out of that northern hollow, on its way down to the river. I would twirl around, willing it to lift me off the ground. It made me feel connected to the forces of nature. I still do it sometimes when no one else is around."

I turned to gauge her reaction. She was looking at me with genuine interest.

"Did the wind ever pick you up off the ground?" she asked.

I was caught off guard by that question and took a moment to settle on an answer.

"No, but I used to have dreams about riding the wind."

She smiled and turned to the tiger lilies that Jonah was sniffing. "Did your mother plant these?"

I rushed over to retrieve Jonah's lead and pulled him out of the flower bed.

"Yes. It's nice that they left them alone," I said.

She studied me silently for a moment.

"Ready to head back?" she asked.

I followed her to the sidewalk. She walked at a brisk pace that matched mine and flashed me a smile.

"You have your mother's dark eyes and golden-brown hair."

I nodded. "Yes, but my father's suntanned complexion. My mother had very fair skin."

She looked at me oddly, and I thought she was going to ask about my father, so I blurted out the first thought that came to me.

"My mother was wary of you, as I recall."

I was instantly sorry I said it, but she just laughed good-naturedly.

"She wasn't alone. I was an enigma to small town women – single, financially independent. Much like you are now," she pointed out.

"It was more than that," I told her. "I recall that whenever you would approach me to talk after church, she would always come over and hustle me away from you." My writer's curiosity was overpowering the manners my mother had instilled in me – an area of parental guidance in which she had excelled. "There were whispers in school that you were some sort of mystic."

She laughed again. "I studied psychology like you, Ruby. But I will admit to being fascinated by the mystical aspects of life, just as you feel drawn to women's issues. I read your book of essays. It's an interesting exposition on the status of women in this world. *The Curse of Eden.*"

That explained how she knew my current last name. I had focused on how women have been treated as secondary since the story of the Garden of Eden, and had showcased strong women from history who had been downplayed by male historians. My agent had managed to get several of the essays published in prestigious magazines. Then he shrewdly solicited jacket blurbs from some powerful, well-known women and nominated the collection for a Pulitzer, in the criticism category. To my surprise, it won, which greatly increased the buzz around the book and the number of sales.

The Pulitzer had ensured the success of my next two books, the first of which was a true crime novel focusing on an infamous local woman who had murdered her infant daughter because her husband longed for a son. The third book was an historical thriller called *The Desert Queen*, which was currently sitting on the New York Times Best Seller List. The money was providing a better lifestyle than I had ever been accustomed to, like the Jaguar and the nice house. Having a savvy agent ranks right up there with having a man who knows what he's doing in bed.

"I've also read your new novel. Very entertaining, but a departure from your first two books, and an unusual choice to write about the Queen of Sheba."

"I became fascinated with her when I was researching my first book. She was an extraordinarily powerful woman for her day, and yet there was very little written about her. I was inspired by Philippa Gregory's red and white queen novels, in which she did a very admirable job of showcasing the strong queens of medieval England, and thought perhaps I could do the same for Sheba."

"You added some entertaining elements." That mysterious smile again.

"I'm glad you think so."

"I noticed in the credit section that you interviewed Sophia Russo for your essay on Sheba."

"That's right."

Sophia Russo was a renowned Egyptologist and professor emeritus at the American University in Cairo, whom I had interviewed on the phone and by email. She had ties to the area through her late husband, who was once on the faculty of Washington University in St. Louis.

"Are you aware that she's speaking at a local college tomorrow evening?" she asked.

"Yes. It's the kickoff of the annual speaker series at Lewis and Clark College. She emailed to let me know she was coming and invited me to attend."

"So you're going then?"

"I am. Are you?"

"Yes."

We had reached my car and Jonah jumped up on her to kiss her face before I put him in the back seat, and I was struck again by how both Jonah and I had so easily accepted her into our inner circle.

"Where are you staying?" I asked. "Perhaps we could ride together."

"I still own the same house, at the end of Marigold Lane." It was one of several hollows that lead back into the bluff side of town. "But I'll be coming from somewhere else tomorrow evening. Perhaps I'll see you there?"

I nodded and hesitated for just a second before reaching inside the console of my car for my wallet and digging out a card that had my personal email and cell phone number on it. I'm a private person and generally use the cards for business purposes, but it was rare that I met a woman I liked so much.

"If your plans change, or if you'd like to get together again for a cocktail or another walk?" I held out the card.

"Thank you." Her smile was genuine as she took the card and read it. "That's an unusual graphic."

She meant the brilliant ruby on the left side of the card, embedded in the hilt of a dagger.

"Yes. The artist who designed the card thought it would be a unique touch - a play on my name."

She held my eyes for a moment and I thought she might say something more. Instead, she squeezed my arm. "Take care. We'll meet again."

And with that she turned and walked down the street. I had intended to offer her a ride. I watched her disappear behind the church's rectory, then my gaze was drawn back up to the house on the bluff.

The sun had disappeared and the house was shrouded in dark clouds that gave it an ominous appearance. As I stood there looking, a gradual feeling of dread came over me.

I got behind the wheel, hoping to beat the storm back to my house, but I couldn't shake the dark mood that was impinging on me. As I exited town and passed the Wind Rivers Condos on the riverfront, the sky turned suddenly black. I wouldn't recognize the irony in that until later.

*****

Chapter 3

"The Queen of the South! Do you believe she really existed?"

Sophia Russo paced the front of the Ann Whitney Olin Theatre. There was a hint of mischief in her smile as she surveyed the full house. I knew her to be in her 70s. She had a sleek, graceful way of moving. Her hair - naturally white now, was still thick against pale skin. Her voice held a slight Greek accent.

"Was she a beautiful, rich and powerful ruler from an exotic land?" She paced back over to the podium. "Did she travel across the desert to witness firsthand the wisdom of the great King Solomon?" She leaned across the podium to address the audience conspiratorially, "Did Solomon trick her into his bed by feeding her a peck of pickled peppers?"

I laughed along with the rest of the crowd, and she joined in.

"She is referred to by several major ancient sources, including the Ethiopian Kebra Negast, or the Glory of Kings, which gives us the account of Solomon's seduction. She is also referred to in a

Pulitzer prize-winning essay collection and a bestselling novel by Ruby January, who is sitting in the audience this evening."

She smiled and pointed at me and the audience turned to have a look and applaud politely. I gave a little wave and waited for Sophia to continue.

"For those of you who are not familiar with the story, Solomon feasts her with spicy food to induce her thirst and compels her to vow she will not take anything from his palace. She agreed to his request, but upon waking with a burning thirst, helped herself to a jar of water by her bed – water being the most precious commodity of all. Solomon then emerged from the shadows, revealed her mistake and compelled her to spend the night in his bed in 'reparation.' He could teach these modern men a thing or two about the art of seduction, do you not agree?"

Another ripple of quiet laughter. She picked up a clicker from the podium and set a PowerPoint presentation in motion on two large screens, one on each side of the stage, and the lights grew slightly dimmer. "These are the remains of the temple that were uncovered in the Yemeni province of Marib. The temple is believed to have been established circa 10th century BC. When a team of archaeologists began excavation of the site in 1988, they uncovered columns marking the entrance to the 'Throne of Bilquis,' which is associated with the name of Sheba. They have since uncovered an impressive collection of artifacts. These archaeologists believe they are on the path to uncovering the secrets of the Queen of Sheba. But who was this mysterious woman?"

I relaxed into my seat as she outlined what the ancient tomes report. Most of what she was saying I was already familiar with, but Sophia Russo had a commanding presence and a very engaging speaking style. I also happened to know that her son had been one of those archaeologists she was referring to, but she did not mention that to the audience, and for good reason.

I felt a sudden shiver go up my spine - the tickling sensation you get when it feels like you're being stared at from behind. It felt like it was coming from the left side of the room, and I slid down into my seat and shot a discreet glance over my left shoulder. Like a magnet my eyes were drawn to a big man several rows behind me and my breath caught in my chest, because I recognized him from my dream, even though I'd never seen him before in person. He had dark blond hair, worn rather short, and he sat with a military bearing. He was wearing a crisp white shirt, in contrast to his tanned skin, but it was his eyes that captured my attention. Even from a distance I could see that they were green, just like in my dream, and they were staring right at me.

I stubbornly returned his stare, unwilling to break eye contact first, which apparently amused him because his mouth eased slowly into a smile of pure male self-assurance. Finally, I relented and broke contact because it was rude to be turned around, but for the rest of the lecture I felt off-balance. When it was over I risked another glance and found that he was gone. I scanned the room in earnest as people piled into the aisles, but he was nowhere to be seen. I also did not see Jewel Alexander.

I retrieved my bag from under the seat and headed into the center aisle. A couple of people stopped me for an autograph, which I politely supplied while making my way toward the front, wanting to speak with Sophia. She was chatting with some of the college administrators when she caught my eye and called out to me, "Ruby!" and motioned me ahead. I stepped to the front and extended my hand.

"Dr. Russo, it's a pleasure to finally meet you in person. I enjoyed your lecture very much."

"I am so pleased to hear it," she said as she accepted my handshake. "I was hoping to have a word with you in private. Is there someplace we might meet for a few moments when I am finished here?

"The library would be good. It's just across the old fountain court out front. I'll meet you under the stained-glass window in the front of the reading room."

"I hope that it is not an imposition?"

"None whatsoever. Please take your time."

I turned and made my way to the front doors and out into the night. A breeze broke through the heavy night air and whipped my skirt lightly against my thighs. I held my bag over my shoulder with a firm grip and headed across the dimly lit court, passing well-tended landscaping and a large sculpture of Sacajawea, the Shoshone Indian woman who guided Lewis and Clark on their expedition westward.

I saw no one else, but I couldn't shake the feeling that I was being watched, just like inside the theater. I glanced around the courtyard one more time, but I was alone with only the soothing murmur of water from the fountain breaking the silence.

Reid Memorial Library stood directly in front of me, its aged stone walls illuminated by moonlight. I made my way inside and went straight to my favorite table underneath a large stained-glass window depicting a beautiful female angel in a green robe. I searched in my bag for some articles I was reading in research of my next book and busied myself highlighting interesting passages. I had earned my bachelor's degree at this college and the quiet, studious atmosphere of the library absorbed me, as always, so I didn't notice Sophia until she was standing across the table from me. She regarded the angel thoughtfully.

"What a beautiful window," she remarked.

"I know," I said. "I love stained glass, and something about that angel speaks to me. I actually wrote a good deal of *The Curse of Eden* at this table."

"Did you?" She smiled at me and turned back to the window to study the picture to the side of the angel, depicting two young figures singing from a missal.

"This library used to be a chapel back in the days when the college was still Monticello Female Seminary. Please, sit down, Dr. Russo." I pointed to the seat across from me.

"Thank you," she said as she took a seat. "But please call me Sophia."

"All right," I smiled.

"I have read some of the history of this college," she said. "It was touted as the first female seminary in the West."

"Yes. Back in those days, most schools for girls were merely finishing schools. But Monticello offered women a bona fide higher education. The principal, Harriet Haskell, was an early advocate of sports for women and was quite popular among the students."

There was once again a hint of mischief in her eyes, and I noticed up close now that they were a fine shade of blue grey with faint laugh lines that hinted at a former beauty, now faded.

"Apparently, she is still quite popular among the students," she supplied.

"Oh, you've heard the ghost stories!" I said in surprise. There had been reports over the years of people seeing Harriet Haskell or being tapped on the shoulder to find no one behind them. It amused me to hear it mentioned by someone of Sophia Russo's stature. "It's part of the college lore, but I've never placed much stock in ghost stories. I came here for the ambience. It seemed appropriate to write about the struggles of women in this former sanctuary of female education. And this angel was a muse of sorts for me. I did some of my best writing here."

She turned to regard the window for a moment, then turned back to me with a smile.

"I'm so proud of you, Ruby, and how well your writing career is going."

"Thank you. That means a lot to me, coming from you," I said sincerely.

"It's interesting to me that you earned your master's in psychology. Did that influence your decision to write?"

"Yes, particularly the psychology of women. In the scriptures we learn that because of Eve's mistake in eating the forbidden apple and offering it to Adam, we've been cursed to desire men, who will rule over us. They both sinned and were given consequences, but an emphasis on Eve's mistake over Adam's was often used down through the ages to subjugate women to an extreme amount."

"And yet there is some truth to that 'curse,' as you put it. Most women seek a man who will fulfill their desire - some women to ecstasy, but some to their ruin."

"No doubt," I agreed. I returned her smile without further comment and imagined we were both wondering about each other's experience with men.

"I was hoping you might take me to lunch in Grafton while I am here," she finally said. "I passed through there when I was younger and I have a desire to see it again."

"Of course, I'd be delighted." Very pleased, actually. There was something I wanted to speak to her about, and a relaxing lunch might be a more suitable opportunity. "Are you free tomorrow? We could take a drive through town, then have lunch somewhere. Aeries Winery has good food, and their deck has one of the most stunning views of the area."

"That sounds perfect. Could you pick me up around 11:00? I am staying at the Beall Mansion here in La Vista."

"I know the place. Do you need a ride there now? My car is right outside."

"No, that is very kind of you, but I have promised to have a nightcap with some of the professors here." She stood gracefully and gave me an enigmatic smile. "I shall look forward to our day together with great anticipation."

"As will I."

I watched her exit the library and decided I was done for the night. I gathered my things and started for the front exit. Halfway across the room I stopped abruptly and turned to have a look around. The feeling that I was being watched had rushed back over me, stronger than ever but, as far as I could tell, I was alone in the library. I decided it was the talk of ghosts and shook it off.

I left the building, following the sidewalk to the north parking lot. As I approached my car, I noticed a familiar figure leaning against it, wearing an emerald green summer dress with gold, strappy sandals.

"Hello, Jewel."

"Good evening, Ruby. I'm sorry that I missed you in the lecture. I spotted where you were sitting but got caught up talking with someone when the lecture ended. When I looked for you, you were gone."

"I met with Dr. Russo briefly afterwards. Did you enjoy the lecture?"

"Very much. I've heard her speak before, in Cairo. I came here with a friend, but he got called away. I was wondering if you could give me a lift back to my car. I left it in a lot outside of town."

"Sure, no problem."

I hit the keyless remote and she smiled at me and moved around to the passenger door to climb in. I fired the engine and shifted into gear. As we rolled past the library, the stained-glass window, lit up in the night sky, caught my attention and I smiled to myself.

"What?" Jewel asked.

"I was just thinking about my conversation with Sophia. Have you ever met her?"

"I have, actually. What did you talk about?"

"Oh, the usual topics with a distinguished academic... men, angels, ghosts."

She laughed along with me and I was struck again by how comfortable I felt with her. There was a familiarity about her, almost like what I felt with my best friend, Nicole, but we had been close since we were children growing up on the same street in Grafton, and our bond is unshakeable.

"Where is your car?"

"It's in the rest stop underneath the Piasa Bird."

It made sense, as that was a parking area close to the entrance to town, but my gut clenched with anxiety and we rode for a few moments in silence. As we hit the entrance to the River Road, I sneaked a glance at her. She politely pretended not to notice.

A moment later, I turned into the rest stop. There was only one car on the lot – a classic Aston Martin. I pulled in next to it.

"I like your car."

"It's very James Bond, don't you think?" she said with a contagious grin. "I bought it years ago and kept it in my garage in Grafton."

I nodded and returned her grin, but my gaze was captured by the large painting of the Piasa Bird on the bluffs, illuminated by spotlights. The Piasa Bird is a local Native American legend. The painting had been spotted by Father (Pere) Jacques Marquette, for whom the state park is named. He was an early explorer to the area, and was astounded by the large, colorful graphic on the rock face above several caves as he traveled down the Mississippi. It depicts a fierce-looking, dragon-like creature. The painting is periodically restored and an information kiosk containing the details of the legend had been installed for the benefit of tourists and local history buffs.

"What is disturbing you, Ruby?"

"This is the spot where Rachael fell from the bluffs."

I turned to search her gaze and had the distinct impression she was aware of that. It would be an easy piece of information to pick up. The story had run in the local newspaper and I imagined people still talked about it.

"What was she doing up there?"

"I have no idea. Rachael was not a hiker, like I am. If there was anyone with her, they never came forward. The coroner labeled her death "caused by internal injuries sustained in a fall of uncertain origin." The reporter told me he had spoken with people close to her who said she'd been suffering from depression over a love affair and the death of our parents."

"And was that true?"

"To some degree, yes. Rachael was in love with a married man who had no intention of leaving his wife, but he didn't mind stringing her along. She was quite pretty and had a sweet personality, if you recall."

She nodded.

"She was also close to our mother. Pathologically close, in my opinion..." I trailed off.

"Because of your father?" she asked.

I looked at her for a moment. "What do you know about him?"

"I know that he was reclusive and never socialized with people. He didn't even attend school programs when you were the vocal soloist."

I let out a sigh. "He had schizoid personality disorder. I didn't know the name for it until I majored in psychology. I just knew that he ignored me and it was painful."

"But he didn't ignore Rachael?"

I wasn't prepared for this conversation and tried to decide what to say, but she let me off the hook.

"I imagine dealing with the dynamics in your family sharpened your instincts. Sometimes those instincts are trying to tell us things we're not consciously aware of, but sense somewhere deep down inside. You're a psychology major. You know this." She opened the passenger door and turned back to me. "If there's anything you need to talk about, you know where to find me. You're welcome there anytime. And thank you for the ride." She smiled and slid out of the car, made her way to the Aston Martin and climbed in.

My gaze was drawn back up to the fierce dragon on the rocks. I imagined Rachael falling past it and wondered what her last thoughts had been. *Was she terrified?* I hoped not, but it was too painful to think about, so I fired the engine and drove away into the night.

Later, in bed, I fell into a fitful sleep and entered the recurring dream again. In a lucid state, I stood in front of the bluff house looking up at the two-story windows. Inside one I could make out the dark shape of a man, but not his features. I believed he was the source of the paradox of seduction and repulsion.

I resisted the impulse to enter the house and turned to a path that was hidden behind some foliage. Only the locals know about this path that cuts through the bluffs. It was useful if you didn't want your movements detected. I had used it often as a teenager.

Off to the left I saw a man tinkering with a touring class Harley, which would have been out of place if I hadn't known it was a dream. This path was not suitable for motorcycles. It was dark outside, and the path was lit only by moonlight. I stepped over a low stone retaining wall to get a better look. He turned and I recognized my lost love, James 'Jamie' Sinclair.

Against my better judgment, I started towards him, but my attention was caught by a young woman running past us on the path, her long hair streaming behind her. Her fear was palpable, and I vaulted back over the stone wall in pursuit, wanting to help her. My feet pounded the hard, earthen path as I picked up speed, but her pace eluded me.

Suddenly, I was pulled to the side by the man I saw at the lecture, and I tumbled to the ground, off-balance. He hauled me to my feet and our faces were inches apart. My attraction to him was overpowering my senses. He produced a necklace – a brilliant ruby suspended from a gold chain and slipped it around my neck. Then he bent to whisper something to me, but the bells of St. Patrick's began to ring, and I couldn't make out the words.

I awoke with a start, just as I always had at this point. I reached instinctively between my breasts for the ruby but, of course, it wasn't there.

I fell back into the pillows and lost myself in thoughts of the green-eyed man until I was lulled back into sleep. This time I did not dream.

*****

Chapter 4

The historic Beall Mansion is located on 'Millionaire's Row' on 12th Street. It was once the home of Senator Edmund Beall and had been converted into a lodging house combining the very best of antiquity and modern convenience. It was a beautiful example of La Vista in its heyday of wealthy industrialists.

The young woman at the desk confirmed that Sophia was expecting me and directed me upstairs to her room. The door was ajar and, when I knocked, Sophia called out for me to come in. She was in the private bath and I recalled from a tour I had taken that it featured a whirlpool for two, Italian marble floor and a basket light fixture with hand-polished Czechoslovakian crystal. I thought it a setting befitting a woman of Sophia Russo's grace and charm as I wandered over to the west window to enjoy the view of meticulously landscaped grounds and the remains of the original goldfish pond and fountain.

Sophia emerged wearing khaki capris, a white cotton blouse and flat sandals. Her hair was pulled back with a heavy barrette. Perfect for the day at hand, I thought, and hoped I would look that good at her age, if I lived that long.

"Lovely, is it not?" she smiled at me and gestured to the room.

"Yes. You must be very comfortable here."

"I am. Shall we go see where you grew up?"

We headed out and chatted about our respective careers on the drive. With the weather warming back up, the river was once again dotted with boaters — sailboats, water skiers, pontoons, even fishermen in johns. The River Road was once again dotted with bicyclists, joggers, dog walkers and motorcycles.

"This road is a hidden treasure for this area," Sophia commented. "I imagine many of the people who live around here take it for granted."

"I believe so, but not me. It never fails to stir something in me. One of my earliest memories is of my mother bundling us into coats and then into the back seat of my father's Chevy Impala so she could take him to work at a foundry in La Vista and keep his car for the day. I was half-asleep, watching those towering bluffs fly by, enchanted." I turned to her. "You said you passed through Grafton before?"

"Yes, on my way up to Kampsville. You are aware that my late husband, Richard, was an archaeologist?"

I nodded.

"He taught at Washington University for many years and during that period he was involved with the Native American dig up in Kampsville.

"Yes, I'm aware of that old site." It was on the other side of Marquette State Park.

"He was as passionate about archaeology as I am about the history of Egypt," she said. "We were a good match."

"How did you meet him?"

"Through a faculty exchange program. He came to teach in Cairo for awhile."

"Was it love at first sight for you?" I was genuinely interested.

"No. It was always more of a friendship love between us."

I slowed down as we entered Grafton. We took a leisurely drive through town and she commented on how much it had changed over the years, just as she had heard. Then we started up the uber steep hill above the Grafton Marina that leads to Aeries Winery. I pointed to the condos on our left.

"That's where my elementary school was, in that valley right over there. After the Great Flood, they demolished it and rebuilt it up in the bluffs. We used to trudge up this hill to a ball diamond in gym class. Even as a child, it was a hard trek."

"And did you enjoy your time in school there?" she asked.

"Very much. I excelled at academics and school was a haven for me. I participated in performing arts, but I was also very drawn to books. I believe that fire was ignited in me by my fourth-grade teacher, who read to us in a soothing voice while I daydreamed out the window. I've been a reader ever since, and now a writer of books."

We pulled into the parking lot and I turned off the ignition. "Shall we go in?"

There was a good lunch crowd in Aeries, as usual.

"What is that line of people for over there?" she asked, pointing to a small crowd a few hundred yards away.

"That's the Grafton Zipline through the bluffs. Have you ever ridden one?"

"No, but I am sure it is exhilarating. Have you ridden it?"

"Once. And I think once was enough!"

We took a seat on the deck, near the front banister that overlooks Grafton and the river. A large umbrella over our table provided protection from the advancing sun, aided by a slight breeze blowing.

"You did not exaggerate. The view is breathtaking."

"It is," I agreed and took the seat facing west. From up there I could just make out the rooftop of the house above St. Patrick's.

A waitress came with menus and we ordered an appetizer of grilled shrimp, Florentine pizza and a bottle of a good pinot grigio. I tried to keep my eyes from wandering to the bluff house as we munched on shrimp and sipped wine for awhile in companionable silence – another older woman who was easy to be with. I wanted to ask her something, but it was of a very serious nature and I thought perhaps I should wait until we finished eating, so I continued our earlier conversation instead.

"You mentioned your love for Richard was a friendship kind of love. Did you ever experience the other kind...the take your breath away romantic kind?"

She smiled and sipped her wine for a moment as she looked out over the river. "Yes, I did. It is interesting that you brought that up. I wanted to tell you about it. It was when I was still young, before I met Richard. We were not supposed to be together, but when someone like that comes into your life...something that is bigger than you and anything you have ever encountered, it is impossible to resist."

"What was he like?"

She let out a rush of breath. "He was unlike anyone I had ever met before or since. I am past the age of worrying about what people think, so you will forgive me if this sounds immodest, but I was quite beautiful when I was young and he could not resist me either. The forbidden aspect only sweetens the temptation."

It sounded like she had gotten involved with a married man, but a lot of women make that mistake and she had been very young then.

"He had abilities that made Richard pale in comparison," she continued, then watched me silently for a moment. "Do you know what I mean?"

I shook my head, intrigued, but she suddenly shifted gears.

"You were acquainted with my son, David, were you not?"

Here was part of the subject I had intended to bring up later.

"Yes, I was. When you mentioned to me that he was working at the dig in Marib, I thought it would be interesting to interview him for my novel. I reached out to him and he called me. He took a real interest in my book, and we met on Skype to talk several times. We were going to meet in person on his next trip back here, but then he disappeared." I hesitated, then went on. "I had heard they finally discovered his body in Marib. I'm so sorry, Sophia. I liked him very much. We talked about the dangers of that area, but he was very dedicated to his work."

Her eyes were sad and dreamy for a moment. "He was very much Richard's son in that regard. He studied at Washington University, Richard's alma mater, and followed him into archaeology. He even taught on the faculty there for a time. It was fitting that he had Richard's last name - Vaughn. I kept my own last name, because I was already established as a professor when Richard and I met."

"I understand it is believed he was accosted by bandits on the road to the dig." I said.

"That is the official story, yes. It is a common enough occurrence in that lonely region."

"But you don't believe that's what happened?"

"No. I believe he was murdered, and by someone who knew him." She looked at me for my reaction.

"Why do you believe that? There was no mention of homicide in the articles I read."

"I believe they were searching for something. But there is something else you should know first. He was not Richard's son. My lover was his natural father, but he was taken from me before David was born. There are consequences for breaking sacred laws." She took hold of my wrist and gripped it with an urgent pressure. "Never forget that, Ruby."

"I'm not sure what you're talking about, Sophia." *Did she think she had been punished for committing adultery?*

She slumped back into her seat and took a sip of wine.

"Richard raised David as his own son. I watched David carefully for any sign that he was like his father but I saw none. It was very surprising to me, but sometimes genes are recessive and skip a generation, so I watched his daughter, Angelique, as well. But I have never been certain."

This is where I had heard that name. David Vaughn had mentioned his daughter to me.

"There has always been something strange about that girl," she continued. "Her mother is a vain woman who indulges in affairs, and David was not able to spend as much time with Angelique as he would have liked because of the nature of his work. My work kept me from her, as well, along with Cassandra. There is no love between David's wife and me. I think Angelique had a very lonely childhood." She gave me a rueful smile. "I was curious about you, Ruby. Do you need someone to confide in? I want you to know that you can trust me."

"Sophia, what are you trying to say?"

"Do you really not know, Ruby? Did David not tell you?"

She suddenly turned white as a sheet, staring at something over my shoulder. "Oh my God! Marek?"

I turned around and searched the crowd and my eyes were drawn instantly to a handsome male figure across the deck. He was leaning casually against the banister underneath a sprawling tree. He was dressed in a long-sleeved white shirt tucked into tight tan trousers with knee-high boots – completely wrong for the weather. His hair was shoulder-length, dark gold, and he was staring straight at Sophia with a mysterious smile on his face.

"Oh my God!" she said again and I heard the crash of her wine glass on the deck and turned back to see that she was clutching her left arm.

"Sophia! Are you all right?"

She tried to rise out of her chair and instead slipped down onto the deck in a heap, and I rushed around the table in shock. Her face was pale and sweat was beginning to bead on her forehead. I squeezed her hand.

"Sophia, don't move. I'm going to call for an ambulance."

"Ruby," she whispered and I leaned closer.

"David wanted to protect you."

"Protect me from what?"

She was fading fast and it hit me with sudden clarity that she was dying and there wasn't going to be a need for an ambulance. Then a woman knelt beside us and firmly pushed at me to move.

"Get back, sweetie," she said to me. "I'm a registered nurse. I've called 911."

I started to inch back out of the way as the woman grabbed Sophia's wrist to check her pulse.

"Ruby," Sophia whispered and I leaned down to her face. "Find Jericho..."

She trailed off and slipped into unconsciousness and the nurse pushed me back in earnest and started administering CPR. I came to my senses and turned back to find the man again. There was a group of concerned onlookers standing behind us now, but they parted politely when I stared at them pointedly and this time it was my turn to suffer a shock.

Standing in the exact same place was a man of the same build, but completely different looks. He had dark hair in a more contemporary cut, and a darker complexion, but he was wearing the exact same clothing as the other man. He gave me an insolent smile and I somehow understood that he was the man in my dream – the dark shadow in the window of the bluff house. He put his first two fingertips to his brow and then flipped them towards me in a mock salute. I felt like I had been physically struck and fell back on the deck in confusion.

My view was blocked when the hostess on duty appeared to see what was happening, and I stumbled to my feet and pushed my way through the crowd, out into the sunlight, but the man was no longer there. I felt like I was moving in slow motion. Images of Sophia, Angelique and the golden man started swimming through my mind, and I tried to brush them away as I did a visual search of the deck, but the dark man was nowhere to be seen.

And then the hot sun was blinding me, and between that, the wine, the shocking events of the past several moments and, most especially, the odd sensation from when he pointed his fingers at me, I felt lightheaded. The world started spinning and the deck rushed up to meet me.

*****

Chapter 5

I was back in time, up on the Ridge behind Marquette Park, picking wild blackberries with my mother. She was telling me all about the flowers and bushes we saw – something her mother had taught her. Her dog, Bear, accompanied us and I felt genuinely happy in that moment. My mother had an unhealthy desire for attention, which most people close to her indulged, except for me, but on those rare occasions when I could get her alone, she was like a different person. Underneath the need for attention, my mother had so much good in her, and so much strength. She had a way with sick people, old people, babies and animals – anyone seemingly defenseless. It was in her relationships with men where she struggled, and with me.

In the vision, Bear started to bark at something behind us and I turned and saw a shadow looming overhead as the great Piasa Bird flew into view.

"Ruby?" my mother called to me in alarm.

"Ruby? Can you hear me?" The voice was not my mother's.

I opened my eyes and I was back at Aeries Winery. The hostess who had rushed out on deck was hovering over me, and I realized that someone had carried me into the shade and there was a cushion under my head.

"Are you all right, Ruby?"

"Yes, I'm fine, thank you. I think the heat and the shock just got to me."

I remembered signing a copy of my book of essays for her on another outing here but, to my chagrin, I couldn't remember her name.

"Have a drink of water," she said kindly and held a glass to my lips as I sipped.

"Sophia. Where is she?"

"They're loading her into the ambulance. Fortunately, there was one in the area. It usually takes them awhile to get to Grafton. They're taking her to La Vista Memorial."

I sat up as a paramedic approached and squatted down.

"Hi. How are you feeling?" he asked.

He reached for my face to check my pupils, and I did my best to conceal my annoyance. Then he took hold of my wrist for my pulse.

"Is Sophia still alive?" I asked him.

"She's unconscious." His tone was noncommittal — a bad sign. "Are you family?"

"A friend," I said, and brushed his hand away. "I'm fine. Just take care of Sophia." Even as I said it, I knew she was dead and that they had been unsuccessful in attempting to revive her.

"If there's someone close to her, you should call them and have them meet us at the hospital," he told me.

He got up and left and I heard the whine of the ambulance siren as I struggled to my feet.

"Is there someone you would like me to call?" the woman asked.

"She has a granddaughter, but I'm not sure where she lives. Angelique is her name. Angelique Vaughn."

"I know who she is. She's renting one of the condos down at Wind Rivers. I'll call the owner.

He's a friend of mine. We'll track her down – don't you worry." She handed my purse to me. "Are you okay to drive? Do you need someone to take you to the hospital?"

"No, I'm fine, thank you. Can I take care of the check now?"

She waved me off. "No, honey, there's no charge. You take care on the drive."

"Thank you," I said again. "You've been very kind." I forced a smile and made my way across the deck amidst people who had returned to their tables and now politely averted their eyes.

I glanced once more at the table I had shared with Sophia and felt a terrible sense of loss. Somehow it seemed even more significant than when I lost Rachael or my mother. But it wasn't any of them who plagued my mind as I drove stoically past the Wind Rivers Condos, where Angelique Vaughn was apparently staying, and then back down the River Road. I was haunted by the image of my father and the memory of the last time I ever saw him.

*****

Chapter 6

I watched Angelique from my seat in the hospital lobby. She was down the hall speaking in hushed tones with a doctor. She was wearing gray slacks with a black blouse and pumps – all business. A part of me noted with amusement the doctor's mesmerized expression as Angelique leaned towards him and spoke; his solicitous posture as he reached out to squeeze her shoulder. Then she apparently had everything she needed and turned dismissively, walking briskly towards the lobby. He watched her longingly, then noticed me and flashed me an engaging smile – a player.

I stood and faced her as she approached. Her eyes assessed me before she stopped in front of me.

"Angelique, I'm terribly sorry about your grandmother. I admired her very much."

"The doctor said you were with her when she had the heart attack. What were you doing?"

"We were having lunch at Aeries Winery."

"Yes, but why were you with Sophia?"

I took in the guarded look in her eyes and the tone of her voice that was a tad too nonchalant.

For some reason, this mattered to her, but Sophia's words were playing in my head... *David wanted to protect you.*

"I interviewed her for one of my books. I'm a writer."

"I know who you are." Her tone was irritated. "Did she tell you anything interesting?"

I was taken aback by how inappropriate that sounded under the circumstances. I let it hang in the air for a moment, then finally said, "She was an interesting woman. Is there anything I can do for you?"

She seemed at a loss for words, which I was guessing was uncharacteristic for her.

"I understand you're staying at Wind Rivers," I said.

"Yes. I'm an attorney. I have a client who is exploring business opportunities in the area. I'm researching for him."

"What kind of opportunities?"

"Profitable ones."

Smartass. I switched gears. "Will there be a memorial service? I know Sophia had friends in the St. Louis area."

"Yes. I'll arrange for something simple here. There will be something more substantial later in Cairo where the bulk of her friends and colleagues live. If you give me your contact information, I'll let you know when it's finalized."

I dug in my purse for a blank business card and wrote my personal email address on it. I didn't offer my cell number. She accepted it and nodded.

"Well, I won't intrude on your grief any longer. I'm very sorry for your loss." I turned towards the door, but she called out to me.

"Ruby."

I turned back.

She hesitated for a moment, then forced a smile. "Thank you. I'm glad she wasn't alone at the end."

I nodded and walked through the lobby doors out into the brilliant sunlight – a cheery imposter masking over a dark day. As I worked my way across the parking lot, I wondered what Sophia's last words had meant – *Find Jericho*. The city of Jericho? I knew it was the site of frequent archaeological digs. Was there a connection to David Vaughn there?

Images from the day flashed through my mind, but none as strong as the dark-haired man on the deck of the winery...the shadow in the window of the bluff house.

*****

Chapter 7

The next two days were blazing hot. That suited me fine and I holed up in my house laying down some story beats for my next novel.

At the end of the second evening, as the sun was sinking below the river's horizon, I rewarded myself with a swim. My pool is a lush oasis with a waterfall, and Jonah joined me for a couple of laps, then went to roll in the grass and take up a position guarding the grounds.

When I'd had my fill of swimming, I took my cell phone and sat on one of the oversized boulders that overlook the river, to call my son. He had left early for college in northern Illinois, because he was on the soccer team and they had to train hard for a couple of weeks before the season got underway.

His team was going to play an exhibition game on the field at St. Louis University High School in a couple of days and I made plans to go and watch. Then I went inside and checked my email. There was a brief note from Angelique letting me know there would be a memorial service the following evening at St. Patrick's in Grafton, and that she looked forward to seeing me there. The location was surprising, as I had assumed it would be the chapel at Wash U, but I made plans to attend that too.

Then I took a brief shower, blow-dried my hair, slipped on a white silk camisole and tap pants and slid between the sheets. As I drifted into slumber enjoying the smell of coconut shampoo in my hair, a title for my book took form in my mind. In the story of Rapunzel – a fairy tale taught to generations of girls, a beautiful young woman is locked away in a tower out of jealousy for her feminine power, and in Hollywood, a renowned hotel on Sunset Boulevard features a tower in its design. It's loaded with ambience and is legendary as a meeting place for power players in the movie industry. I had become slightly obsessed with it and was considering using it as an initial meeting locale for the main characters. When things settled down, I intended to take a trip to Los Angeles to conduct some research.

There was also another, more famous, tower that was starting to invade my dreams and visions. I wasn't sure what role that might play, but I still had time to let the story unfold in my mind. I fell asleep envisioning the title suspended in the air, shrouded in mystery – *White Tower.*

*****

Chapter 8

The first time I ever sat in a service in St. Patrick's, everything seemed so foreign. My mother had been a lapsed Catholic and decided when I was in the second grade that she should raise us in church, so I had to do some catching up to my classmates who were Catholic. And it was in catechism class on Saturdays that I first became aware of gender issues. The humorless old nuns who drove up from a convent in La Vista to teach us told us that girls should cover their heads with a veil in church because women are subject to men, even though it was no longer an official dogma and most women no longer followed that custom. My seven-year-old sense of justice was affronted by this and the roots of my writing quest were established.

Sitting in a pew at St. Patrick's was nostalgic for me as I watched Angelique on the front row with whom I suspected was her mother, based on their resemblance. I was reminiscing about an Easter service here with my family. My sister and I were dressed alike in brand new white and navy coat dresses, complete with wide-brimmed hats and white gloves. My mother wore an off-white dress and matching pillbox hat with netting – very Jackie Kennedy. My father had attended that service with us, even though he was not Catholic. It had felt like we were a real family, despite a nagging sense that something was not right about my father.

The woman I presumed was Cassandra Vaughn turned to sneak a glance at me and I caught my breath at the naked hostility on her face. There were some radical people from both the liberal and conservative schools of thought who took issue with some of my essays, but even they didn't look at me like that – *at least, not to my face.*

I felt a light touch on my shoulder and turned to see Jewel in the pew behind me. She smiled and winked at me as someone from the faculty at Wash U took the lectern to open the memorial service. I settled in and listened to Sophia's colleagues talk about her devotion to her discipline, her love for Richard and David, and her roots in Athens, where she had grown up with a Greek mother and Italian father.

I was wondering about the mysterious paramour whom she had told me fathered David. I believed he was the man I had seen briefly in the vision at Aeries, and that Sophia had seen him too, setting off her heart attack. I wondered how he had died. I had researched the name Marek. It was

Polish and meant warlike, which didn't really tell me anything.

When the service was over, I slipped out of the pew and genuflected towards the altar. I don't agree with all of the doctrines of the Catholic Church, but I have a healthy respect for tradition. There was no body to view, as Sophia's remains had been cremated, so I made my way outside and decided to wait and have a word with Angelique out of courtesy. I was disappointed to see that Jewel was nowhere in sight. She must have slipped out before the service ended. Her presence had felt comforting to me.

While I waited, I permitted myself a look up at the bluff house. This time, it just looked dignified and non-threatening.

"Es una casa bonita, si?" A deep male voice shivered down the back of my neck from close range.

Pleasantly surprised, I shot back over my shoulder, "Si, muy bonita. Pero mi espanol, no tanto!"

I laughed and turned around smack into the handsome smiling face of the dark man from the deck of the winery. I took an instinctive step back, putting some distance between us.

"I'm sorry," he switched into flawless English with the barest trace of Spanish accent. "Did I startle you? Please forgive me. I was intrigued that you were so intent on my house. Well, it's not *my* house. I'm leasing it temporarily."

I didn't have a clue what to say. I was not prepared to see him in this setting and I gave him a discreet once-over as I struggled to collect my thoughts.

He was beautiful in an animal masculine way. I'm not usually attracted to men with dark hair and eyes (I'm self-aware enough to know why – my father had dark features), but he had a magnetism that was impossible to deny as he stood there with a relaxed smile.

He was tall and lithely muscled, but impeccably dressed in designer clothing, like he had stepped out of a fashion ad for Prada – that bored indifference you see on the faces of male models leaning casually against expensive cars. But there was a decided glint of interest in his eyes as he surveyed me, and he took the initiative to break the growing silence and grabbed my hand in both of his, bringing it up to his lips while holding my eyes with his. Very smooth.

"I'm Rey Ramirez, and I am delighted to meet you, Ms. January, or may I call you Ruby?"

"How do you know my name?"

"Angelique introduced me to your book of essays. I've enjoyed reading it in my spare time. I like women with strong opinions."

I doubted that. Maybe it was the stereotype about Hispanic men, or maybe it was just a vibe from him.

"And how do you know Angelique?"

"She's my attorney. I'm looking for local projects to invest in and she is handling the details for me."

The client.

"And had you met Sophia?" I watched his face carefully.

"I'm afraid I did not get an opportunity."

He was displaying no acknowledgment of the interchange between us at Aeries, so I thought perhaps I had just seen a vision and he hadn't been there. I made a bold move.

"Were you planning to introduce yourself the other day at the winery?"

He looked genuinely confused. "I beg your pardon?"

"I see that you've met my client," came a familiar voice.

Angelique stepped into my line of vision and the woman I assumed was Cassandra Vaughn followed closely behind her. Up close now, I could see that she was indeed an older version of Angelique – probably in her late 50s, but very well preserved and still beautiful. Her complexion was fairer and her hair more of an ash blonde. She was wearing an expensive black suit, with a cami that was cut very low, displaying more cleavage than you normally see at a memorial service.

"This is my mother, Cassandra Vaughn," Angelique said to me, then spoke quietly to her mother, "Ruby January, who was with Sophia when she died."

She had an air about her I can only describe as icy and she looked me up and down with undisguised distaste. I had a gut feeling that she came from money and, as I had not, this was not the first time I'd been looked at that way. In fact, it was triggering an unpleasant memory for me, but I put on my game face.

"Mrs. Vaughn, I'm very sorry for your loss."

She completely ignored me and instead laid her hand on Ramirez's arm in a familiar manner and whispered something in his ear. Then she turned and walked away.

"Please forgive my mother," Angelique said to me. "She doesn't handle grief well, and she's still recovering from my father's death."

I didn't believe for a minute that she was grieving for Sophia, but I deferred to decorum and shrugged my shoulders. "We all handle grief in different ways."

"It was very kind of you to come," she said. "Once again, I'm glad you were with Sophia at the end – that she wasn't alone."

"I was a bit surprised by the venue. I had thought the service might be held at the chapel at Wash U," I commented.

"I did inquire, but the chapel is booked up months in advance. And I thought it might be fitting to hold it here in Grafton, where Sophia left this earth. She was raised Greek Orthodox, but her husband came from a Catholic family." She glanced at Ramirez and then back at me. "I'm afraid we need to get going. My mother is waiting. Would you like to join us for a drink, Ruby?"

I thought I caught something half-hearted in the tone of her voice, like she'd prefer that I didn't. That was okay with me. The thought of having a drink with Cassandra Vaughn was not appealing and I had something else in mind.

"Thank you, no. There is something else I need to do."

"That's okay. I'm sure we'll see each other again. Rey?"

Ramirez, who had been quietly studying me, gave her a devastating smile, then turned back to me. "Actually, Angelique has planned a cocktail party to introduce me to some of the real estate players in the area. We had already set it in motion before her grandmother's untimely passing." He pointed over his shoulder. "We're having it up at the house on Friday at 6:00. We'd both love it if you would come. Wouldn't we, Angelique?"

"Of course. I should have thought of it myself." Her smile did not reach her eyes.

"You've been distracted. I'm sure Ruby understands. We would both be disappointed if you didn't come, Ruby. Will you join us?"

The house.

"Well, I wouldn't want to disappoint you both. I'll see you then. Thank you."

"Until then." He shot me the same devastating smile, then put a solicitous hand on the small of Angelique's back and steered her towards the parking lot.

I stood in the growing twilight and watched them climb into a black Ferrari and drive away, then made my way to my car. I wasn't certain I wanted to see any of them again, but before I did there was someone I wanted to talk to first. I pointed my car in the direction of Marigold Lane.

*****

Chapter 9

I hadn't been on this road since I was in high school, but I remembered hiking through the creek bed that had chiseled the hollow into the bluff with a girl from school. I found the house at the end of the road - a simple cottage-style structure with flowering bushes and a front porch overlooking the gurgling creek. Nice. She came to the open door before I even knocked, a smile on her face.

"Ruby! Come in."

I stepped through the threshold into a living room cooled by a ceiling fan. Even in the subtle lamplight I could see that the furnishings were mostly antiques – expensive-looking pieces. A finely-woven, brightly-colored rug adorned natural hardwood flooring. The centerpiece of the room was a stone fireplace that I imagined was wood-burning.

"I hope I'm not intruding," I said.

She just smiled and shook her head. "Of course not. I'm glad you're here. I made a pitcher of white sangria earlier today. Sound good?"

"Sounds great."

"Make yourself at home. I'll be right back."

She disappeared through a doorway and I busied myself checking out the books in the built-in cases. You can tell a lot about a person by their books. There were several on dreams, and *Interior Castle* by the Catholic mystic, Teresa of Avila. There was a good deal of Jung, and a mix of history, classic literature, poetry and collections of essays, including mine. Some of those books were leather-bound first editions. She had money from some source. Family, maybe? Although that wasn't typical for a military family.

"Let's sit out on the porch," Jewel said as she re-entered the room.

She was carrying a bamboo tray with a pitcher and glasses and I moved to get the door for her. We settled into big cozy wicker chairs with colorful cushions and I kicked off my sandals and stretched out my bare legs. We sipped sangria for a moment.

"Mmmm, really good," I told her. Fresh apples, strawberries and lemons complemented a crisp white.

The steady hum of cicadas was punctuated by the chirp of crickets. The sounds of August. Ever so faintly came the trickle of water over stones from the creek.

"It's very peaceful back here, much like my place up in the bluffs," I told her.

"Yes, I've always enjoyed this secluded little spot."

I smiled as June bugs lit up the front yard. It was late in the season for them.

"Rachael and I used to catch lightning bugs in glass jars and release them back into the night sky. Life is much simpler when you're a child."

"No doubt," she said. "Were you and Rachael close?"

"I thought so, but girls who have a terrible secret, like Rachael, have walls in place. They don't let anyone get too close. She earned straight A's in school, and she was a cheerleader. I looked up to her. But I realized towards the end that I didn't know her as well as I'd thought, even though we shared a double bed for years."

Jewel just smiled faintly and waited.

"People think that sisters are naturally close, and I thought that was the way it should be, but I believe I have a strength that Rachael was lacking. Rachael was the good girl, the obedient girl. I was a good girl, too, but I have a very strong independent streak."

I looked at Jewel and she met my eyes but remained silent. I had become cautious about sharing myself with people but I was in deep now and decided to trust her with the rest of it.

"When I was fifteen, I came home for a break from working the annual Labor Day picnic at St. Pat's with my mother and sister. We always worked the iced tea service, but I had also helped chop green peppers for salads in the kitchen. To this day, the sight and smell of green peppers takes me back to that day." I paused for a moment, then went on. "My father, of course, never attended. He was sitting at the kitchen table drinking beer when I got home. When I walked around him to get a cold drink from the fridge, he did the unthinkable. He pulled out his wallet, showed me his cash, and offered me some to go upstairs with him."

I didn't look at Jewel, just stared out at the creek and continued.

"At first, I thought he was trying to make a joke, albeit a very sick, inappropriate joke. That's what you tell yourself in a situation like that, because your mind can't make sense of it. But when I tried to walk away, he reached out and tried to pull me to him. I shoved him so hard he fell out of his chair. I told him if he ever touched me again, I'd go straight to the police. And then I left him on the floor in a stupor and went back to the picnic and worked another shift."

"Did you tell anyone?" she asked.

"Yes. Later that night, I told my mother. And that's when Rachael broke down in tears and said he had molested her several times but she had been too afraid to tell. Our lives fell apart after that. My mother divorced him, ostensibly because of the abuse but, as it turned out, she had developed a close friendship with one of his coworkers, and she moved into his house. My mother didn't have the means to make it on her own. They eventually got married. I never blamed him. He was a nice man who tried to be fatherly to us."

Jewel nodded her understanding.

"I understood my mother getting divorced; under those circumstances, I would have done the same thing. But she didn't press charges against him. It's a no-win situation. She avoided the public shame, but he got to keep our house. We had to leave our friends, move in with the boyfriend and finish high school in another district. I had just successfully auditioned for the group that produced the high school musicals, which meant the world to me. There was no program at the new school and those dreams got lost in the turmoil, as did Rachael's dream of going to medical school. We were all lost in our own private hurt."

I took a sip of my sangria, then went on. "So, I did what girls do in that situation. I turned to a boy for comfort – an older college boy. I gave him my heart and my virginity, but when he graduated he married the girl his parents had picked out for him – a girl who had attended the same private Catholic schools, and whose parents were friends with his parents. His mother didn't think I was good enough for him, and she had a lot of sway over him, as he was going into their family business. That's why I set my dreams aside and got married right out of high school. Between the pain of losing him and the tragedy of my childhood, I was lost and needed someone to anchor me. Chase offered me that anchor. And then I got pregnant right away and that changed my priorities."

"Did you see your father after that?" Jewel asked.

"Not for several years. But like many girls with that experience, I wanted to somehow fix it. Eventually I worked up the courage to confront him. I wanted him to say he was sorry so I could forgive him and we could try to build a real relationship."

"But he wouldn't admit to it?"

"No. I didn't understand the depth of denial a person with those issues is hiding beneath. A sudden, forceful confrontation can do more harm than good. I wanted to get the truth out in the open between us, because my family was all about the secrets, but he just kept saying that none of it ever happened. It was salt in an open wound, so I told him we had nothing further to discuss and left.

"Did you ever see him again?" she asked.

"No." I looked her in the eye. "He had a stroke and died that night."

"Are you carrying a burden of guilt for his death, Ruby?"

"No. I hope he made his peace with God, but it's not my fault that he couldn't handle being confronted with his actions."

She nodded. "Is that what you came here to talk about tonight?"

"No, but you already had some insight into that situation, and I believe you and I are going to be close friends. Somehow it just seemed right to tell you all of this." I hesitated a moment. "Like I said, there were whispers about you having some sort of special ability, something about visions. Is that true?"

I turned to look at her. She seemed to be choosing her words carefully.

"I have a strong interest in altered states of consciousness and extrasensory perception," she said. "I believe all people are born with a certain amount of it, but a few rare people are born with a special gift for it. Why are you asking, Ruby? Have you had some sort of unusual experience?"

"I've had some odd dreams — lucid dreams in which I sometimes saw things that hadn't happened yet, or that had already happened but I didn't know about in real life. A couple of times I've seen something while awake. I guess you would call those visions."

"How long has that been happening?"

"It started when I was a young girl."

"Did you tell anyone?" she asked.

"Yes. My mother."

"And how did she react?"

"Not well. In fact, the dream I shared with her seemed to upset her a great deal. She said I should learn to ignore it and it would eventually go away. She told me I must never tell anyone. She was adamant about that. I was already a little frightened by it and her anger upset me even more. My mother and Rachael had a close, secretive bond that made me feel like an outsider. I wanted my mother to love me, and this seemed to drive her further away."

"So, you repressed your perception?"

"Yes," I nodded.

"And did it go away?"

"Pretty much. Until recently."

"What's been happening recently?" she asked.

"I've been having a recurring dream about a woman who is in trouble, but I don't know who she is. I don't know if it means anything. Maybe it's just a strange dream. The mind is a complicated instrument and we all have strange dreams that don't make sense. Most of them we never even remember."

"That's true," she agreed. "It might not mean anything, but if you'd like to explore it in hypnosis sometime, I'll be glad to work with you. I do have some experience with that."

"I'll keep that in mind." I hesitated again. "Do you know Rey Ramirez?"

"I know who he is, but I am not personally acquainted with him. Why do you ask?"

I shook my head. "Just something I believe I saw in a vision."

"Be careful not to ignore what you see in your visions. Visions are much less ordinary than dreams. Would you like to tell me about it?"

"No, I'm all talked out for now." I slipped on my sandals and stood up. "Would you like to come to my house for dinner tomorrow? Say 6:00? Maybe we can talk some more then."

"I'd like that," she said.

I told her how to find my house and stepped off the porch.

"Oh. Does Jericho mean anything to you?" I asked her.

"The city?"

"Well...

"Or the man?"

"The man?" I asked.

"Yes. Derek Jericho. He was engaged to David Vaughn's research assistant, Melanie Mayhall. She disappeared shortly before David. I don't believe she's ever been heard from again."

I took a moment to digest that.

"Do you know where I could find him?" I asked her.

"It shouldn't be difficult. He lives in St. Louis, in the private residences penthouse of the Chase Park Plaza."

"How do you know that?" *Writer's curiosity.*

"David Vaughn was a friend of mine," she said with a mysterious smile.

Interesting.

"Good night, Jewel."

"Good night, Ruby. I'll see you tomorrow."

I drove away into the night. By the time I got home, I was relaxed and looking forward to Max's soccer game the next day. I punched in the alarm code and stepped through the side door. Instantly, the hairs on the back of my neck stood up. Jonah was not at the door to greet me and he always meets me at the door. And someone had been inside my house. I could feel it. The house was lit dimly by moonlight through certain windows. No one was in sight and nothing appeared amiss on the surface, but my instincts were on hyper alert.

I slipped off my heels and padded barefoot through the darkened rooms. I longed for the blade in the console of my car, but instead moved forward for the weapon in my bedroom. As I passed my study, something caught my eye. A drawer in my desk was open, ever so slightly. I hadn't left it that way. I'm fastidious about closing things – a tic I picked up from my mother, who had been obsessive about neatness.

I reached the staircase and moved stealthily upward, the moonlight through the second story transom lighting my way. I quieted my mind and concentrated on the presence I had sensed in the house. There was a lingering shape of a man, although it was fuzzy and I couldn't make out any details. I moved steadily towards the master bedroom.

When I reached the doorway, my heart leapt into my throat. Jonah was lying on my bed. I could see him through the ornamental iron railing. I couldn't tell if he was breathing.

I moved quickly towards the bed, stopping before I reached it to bend down and make sure no one was hiding under it. It's that childhood fear we have that someone is under there, but in a situation like this, it was a real possibility.

"Jonah," I whispered.

No response. I reached behind the nightstand for the holster bolted to the frame and slid out my handgun – a 9 mm Beretta Storm Compact - a gift from Nicole, disengaged the safety and racked the slide. I had decided it was a more sensible hiding place than the drawer of the nightstand, where a burglar would look first, and more reachable if I were awakened by an intruder. I had to keep it somewhere, and that location seemed to make sense. I'm not really into guns – I'm more of a blade person, but Nicole's father was a former Marine and had insisted we learn how to shoot. Nic had really taken to it and had persuaded me to keep a gun so we could shoot together at a range. I sent her a mental kiss.

I kept the Beretta ready in one hand and reached for Jonah with the other. He was warm and his chest was rising rhythmically. I felt a dizzying surge of relief and leaned down to kiss his face. He opened his eyes and looked up at me sleepily. I felt his nose to see if it was dry, meaning he might be sick, but it was moist. He stretched and jumped off the bed like he was just taking a nap, except that he always wakes up when I pull in the driveway and meets me at the door, without fail.

I took the Beretta and proceeded to systematically check every room in the house, and every hiding spot in each room, with Jonah following along with me. I found a closet door that was not properly closed and a shoebox in that closet that was on the wrong shelf. I also found another drawer that was not closed properly, but the intruder was no longer present, and nothing was missing. Someone had made a concerted effort to conceal their search. I wondered how he had entered the house with the alarm set. There was no sign of forced entry, but I was certain a stranger had invaded my private sanctuary.

I felt terribly violated, like the night I got mugged for my purse on a pharmacy parking lot when I was seven months pregnant with Max, which didn't stop the guy from shoving me down onto the asphalt pavement. That incident had influenced me to carry a weapon in remote areas. After a moment of shock, I had realized I still had my keys in my other hand. I climbed into my car and chased the guy to the edge of a woods, where he entered and disappeared. Lucky for him, because I just might have run him down for endangering my unborn child. There is no force stronger than maternal instinct.

I felt something like that towards my dog and a part of me regretted there was no one to chase this time. I settled for changing the alarm code and kickboxing the bag in the private gym I'd set up in an extra bedroom. When I was spent, I climbed into bed with Jonah and put the Beretta back into its holster, situated within easy reach from my pillow.

The workout had tired me out. As I started to fade towards sleep, I concentrated on plans for the next day. Max's soccer game was being played in proximity to the Chase Park Plaza, so I determined to try to look up Derek Jericho. There was an image that came into my mind when I thought about his name. It was the green-eyed man from my dream – the same man I'd seen at Sophia's lecture. As I drifted off to sleep, something about him made me feel protected...and strangely in danger.

*****

Chapter 10

The next morning, I took a moment to Google Derek Jericho. All I came up with were a couple of articles from the *St. Louis Business Journal* detailing some investments by Blue London, a venture capital firm. The articles portrayed him as a savvy investor, whose advice was sought by both the old and new money crowds. He had an office in the tony Clayton business sector of St. Louis, but the home office was in London, England. I assumed the Blue part was a reference to blue chip. One article was accompanied by a photo that revealed he was indeed the man from my dream, and Sophia's lecture.

A cool front had passed through in the night, which was good news for the game. I dressed in lightweight, khaki capris that hit mid-calf (I hate those tacky knee-length capris. No one looks good in those.), a white, scoop-neck midriff top and brown leather sandals. Just to be safe, I dropped Jonah off with Nicole. I wasn't quite ready to leave him alone in the house yet.

It was a pleasant day out, for late August, and there was a decent gathering of spectators on the side of the field at SLU High. I felt relaxed and happy to be seeing Max play again. I didn't know anyone on the sidelines, as I didn't see these college parents very often. Okay with me. I'm friendly to people, but I don't feel the need to chat in those situations. I'm happy to say hello, make a little small talk and watch the game, but I happened to be standing next to a mother who did not share that desire. She proceeded to tell me all about her son, his soccer career and his plans after college. She was not deterred when I stopped participating so I could watch Max make a nice pass and set up a goal for a teammate.

"There's my Jason," she told me proudly as her son passed in front of us. "Which one is yours?"

I had been watching Max launch up into the air in an attempt to kick the ball. At the same time, an opponent went for the ball with his head and Max's cleat accidentally clipped him, and they both went down on the ground. Max had a reputation as a clean player who had spent very little time in the penalty box, and he got up and went to offer a hand up to the other player, who ignored his offer and stood up and socked him in the jaw. Max socked him right back and they went back down to the ground, trading punch for punch. Unfortunate timing.

"That's mine over there – number 17," I told her. She looked at me suspiciously, like the woman at the park when I intervened for Jonah. I didn't blame my son for defending himself, but they were both ejected from the game, of course – a first for Max.

I continued to watch for a while but I didn't know any of the other players, and without Max in the game, and with the pushy mother making her way to a clique of women to gossip and surreptitiously point at me, I decided to make my exit.

I made my way to the rear of the bench and caught Max's attention. He reluctantly got up and walked back to meet me. I could see the anger and frustration written all over him.

"I just wanted to see if there's any possibility of you having lunch with me before you leave town?" I asked.

He shook his head. "I have to stay with the team."

"Okay. Well, I think I'm going to head out. I have some business to attend to."

He nodded and continued watching the action on the field. I knew better than to hug him in this situation or to talk about the ejection until he'd had a chance to shake it off, so I contented myself with drinking in the sight of him for a long moment, his summer tan setting off his blue eyes and blonde, wavy hair. His face was starting to show some evidence of bruising.

"Nice assist. Call me when you get a chance. I love you."

I turned to walk away and he called out to me, "Mom." He walked up and gave me a bear hug. "Thanks for coming."

I kissed his good cheek and squeezed him back. "I'll talk to you later."

I walked briskly towards the parking lot past parents I didn't know. Most paid little attention, except for one dark-haired man I caught staring at me from a stand of trees behind the bleachers. When I reached my car, I glanced back, but didn't see him again.

It was a short drive to the Chase Park Plaza. The Chase is a fabulous hotel with a rich history. It came to prominence in the Great Depression and hosted every U.S. president from the 1920s through the 1990s. Foreign kings and dignitaries had stayed there, along with the biggest celebrities of the day. Sinatra and his Rat Pack used to broadcast from the Chase Club.

I parked in a lot facing the Chase on one side, and Forest Park, which had housed the 1904 World's Fair, on another. I cut through the main lobby and corridor past Café Eau and the Chase Cinemas. There was an air of hushed opulence, accentuated by the click of women's heels on marble as I made my way through a long passage of soaring arched doorways until I reached the entrance to the private residences. Jericho obviously had money.

As luck would have it, the concierge was not at his desk and I took the opportunity to slip into the private elevator and hit the penthouse button. The elevator opened into a small private lobby and I stepped forward and rang the bell. I waited a few moments. No response. I rang again. Still nothing. This day was not turning out as I had hoped.

As I dug in my purse for a card, the image of Jericho pulling me aside in my dream and giving me the ruby necklace flashed into my mind with sudden clarity. I put the blank card back and dug in my wallet for one of the cards with the ruby dagger. I didn't write a note - just slipped it under the door and took the elevator back down.

The ball was in his court.

*****

Chapter 11

I drove back to La Vista with the intention of going home to work on my book before dinner, but first I stopped at the Broadway Market and Café to pick up a few things, including Jonah. The market is owned and operated by Nicole's mother, Jane, and Jane's sister June. Nicole is an architect, and she had rehabbed an historic building on the riverfront and let them have the ground floor. The upper two floors are for her use.

I was browsing the fresh produce when I glanced into the café and saw Angelique sitting at a table reading a book and drinking an iced coffee. It seemed odd to see her there in my best friend's building, even though the market is a very popular business.

I made my way to her table and she looked up and smiled as if she were expecting me. The book she was reading was *The Girl Who Kicked the Hornet's Nest*.

"Hello Angelique. We seem to be running into one another a lot."

"Did you know," she asked without preamble, "that ancient Turkish women formed an army that crushed an invasion from the Caucasus, and that a woman in this army was required to slay a man in battle before she could surrender her virginity?"

"I've read Larsson's trilogy," I responded.

She pointed to a chair and I sat down across from her.

"Interesting initiation into womanhood. Do you suppose that rite is being practiced covertly by any modern-day groups?" she asked.

I didn't respond.

"Those women rejected marriage as subjugation," she went on. "Not much has changed in that regard."

"I think that depends on who you marry. Have you ever been married?" I asked her.

"No. Men are all about conquering women. Just as you pointed out in *your* book, they still rule the world. We must use the power we have been granted - their desire to possess us - as the strongest weapon in our arsenal."

She leaned forward and smiled at me quizzically, and then her smile shifted upwards and morphed into something more seductive.

"My date has arrived," she announced.

I turned, half-expecting to see Ramirez, and struggled to conceal my surprise when I saw Jamie

Sinclair standing behind me. He looked equally caught off guard.

"Ruby. How are you?" he asked, after a moment.

He was dressed in jeans, a button-down shirt and work boots, so he'd probably come straight from a job site. Jamie is the president of a very successful general contracting firm, but he'd worked his way up through the ranks of his family-owned business, starting as a carpenter, and he was still very hands-on.

"I'm fine, Jamie. Are you meeting Angelique?"

"Yes, he is. He's going to show me a property in the neighborhood." She stood up and so did I. "I'll meet you out front, Jamie," she smiled at him.

"Of course." He looked at me uncertainly for a moment, then said it had been nice to see me and made his way to the door.

"I was talking to the colorful lady at the bakery counter," Angelique said. "She told me you're a close friend of Nicole Gordon, who apparently is her niece. She's a talented architect. I've seen some of her work in the area. If you like, you can bring her to the cocktail party. Rey and I would both enjoy meeting her."

"I'll extend your invitation," I returned.

"Wonderful. I'll look forward to seeing you there." She looked after Jamie, then back at me and added, "A man needs a prize to pursue. If he was what you wanted, you should have given him that challenge, in spite of his wife. After all, he was yours before they married, wasn't he?"

I wondered if Jamie had told her that and I took a moment to really look at her. She was wearing jeans and a casual top, and she still looked stunning. I imagined she had little trouble getting men to confide in her. I reached out to lightly touch her arm and look into her eyes for a moment.

"Sometimes what we want and what we really need are two different things, Angie."

The color drained out of her face. "That's the last thing my father said to me before he disappeared."

"Then perhaps you would be wise to honor his memory and remember his advice," I told her. "I'll look forward to seeing you tomorrow, as well."

I headed back for the market and left her standing there. The gloves were definitely off.

"Ruby, there was a woman in here asking about you earlier." It was the colorful lady at the bakery counter – Nicole's aunt, June. The colorful was a reference to her bright red hair with blonde streaks and lively style of dress, which today was a lime green top with green feather earrings. I set my produce up on the counter.

"I know," I told her. "I just ran into her in the café. What did she want to know?"

"Oh, she just mentioned she knew we had a famous author in the area and did I know anything about you. So, I told her how you and Nicole have been friends since you were little."

"You talk too much," said a familiar voice. "She was a stranger."

It was Nicole's mother, Jane, who is June's twin sister, but you'd never know it from looking at them. Jane dresses very conservatively, lets her hair go naturally gray and is all business in the market, where she manages the day to day operations. June does all the baking, recreating the wonderful recipes of Nicole's grandmother.

"Well, she looked like a movie star," June answered. "It never hurts to make famous connections. Maybe she could introduce me to Charlie Hunnam." She winked at me and went to wait on a customer.

Jane shook her head in disgust and I smiled to myself. I'd been watching them bicker since I was a kid. Jane had been a backup mother figure to me during my childhood, taking me to lessons with Nicole to ensure I learned how to swim and skate. She turned back to me.

"Watcha need, hon?"

"I need a couple of good steaks for the grill," I told her.

"The butcher cut some nice rib eyes this morning." She wrapped a couple from the meat counter and started ringing my purchases. "Nic says the theater is coming right along. Wasn't that the contractor I saw in here a few minutes ago?"

She was referring to the Paramount Theatre, a rehab project Nicole and I had developed together on Broadway. We had been able to secure TIF (tax increment financing) money and a block grant to supplement our personal funds, in order to complete the project as a proper luxury-style theater.

"Yes, that was Jamie Sinclair," I answered. "I haven't been by the site lately, but I know Nic is very pleased with the progress."

"Well, people are excited that the Paramount is going to re-open," she smiled at me. "Everyone has fond memories of that place."

Including Nicole and me. We had fallen in love with movies when we saw a re-showing of *Gone with the Wind* there when we were young girls, and we still see movies together on a regular basis. The Paramount would give us a nice local venue in which to do it.

"Shall I put this on your account, hon?"

"Please." I picked up the sack. "I need to run upstairs and retrieve Jonah."

"Nic took them both over to the park for a walk, so he should be tuckered out," she advised me.

I thanked her and headed for the private stairs that lead up to Nicole's second floor studio. The third floor serves as her living space. I stepped inside the studio and was immediately pounced on by Jonah and Ginger, Nicole's golden retriever and Jonah's best friend. They collected my attention, then ran out onto the open balcony to play and I wandered over to Nicole's drafting board, where she was bent over a blueline elevation of the Paramount.

"Everything okay?" I asked her.

"Yes, you know me. I obsess over the details, just like you when you're writing."

Nicole is one of those rare women who looks really good in short hair. Hers is red, like June's, and curls softly around her face. It's a nice contrast to her turquoise eyes, which she plays up with colored pencils, but today she wasn't wearing makeup and I could see the faint freckles across her nose that always take me back to our childhood. Her house had been two blocks down the street from mine and I had spent almost as much time there as I had in my own.

"I saw Jamie downstairs," I told her.

"Oh yeah? How did that go?"

I shrugged. "I didn't really talk to him. He was with someone. A real estate lawyer named Angelique Vaughn. Know anything about her?"

"I've heard her name in certain circles. She normally operates in St. Louis and I think New York, but lately she's been nosing around this area. Do you know her?"

"Sort of. She'd like to meet you. She invited us both to a cocktail party in Grafton tomorrow night. Do you want to go?"

"I don't see why not. Were you planning to go?"

"Yes. Do you know who owns that fancy house on the bluff above St. Patrick's?" I asked her.

"I believe it's an attorney from St. Louis. I've heard he has business interests in several cities and travels a lot. Why do you ask?"

"That's where the party is. Angelique represents the guy who is leasing it. I've never been up there and thought it would be interesting to see."

"Okay," she nodded. I'll pick you up. What time?"

"Starts at 6:00, so any time after that."

I headed for the door and Nic followed me over. The dogs came running out to meet us, but I was distracted by thoughts of Rey Ramirez, and Nicole, who knows me better than anyone, picked up on it.

"What's bothering you? Seeing Jamie?"

I shook my head. I'd fill her in later. "Nothing. Thanks for keeping Jonah. I'll see you tomorrow."

I gave her a quick hug and headed out the door, shifting my attention to my dinner with Jewel. I was looking forward to talking with her again. I believed there was something important that she knew – something she wasn't letting on about yet. I decided to enjoy a good meal and interesting company and see what the evening revealed.

*****

Chapter 12

I mixed up a salad with a mustard vinaigrette, then sprinkled the steaks with garlic salt and drizzled olive oil and sea salt on some fresh asparagus and red bell peppers before tossing them all on the charcoal grill. Then I changed into a sundress. I don't fix dinner for someone else very often and for some reason this seemed like an important occasion. When Jewel arrived, she was also wearing a nice summer dress, so perhaps she did too.

"I brought the rest of the sangria from last night. I hope that's appropriate." She was holding a portable pitcher.

"It's perfect. I just brewed some iced tea. This will be better."

"Let's drink the tea with dinner, and save the sangria for after," she suggested.

"That'll work."

I took the pitcher from her and Jonah came out to meet her.

"You look none the worse for wear, Jonah." She bent down to stroke his coat.

"No, he made a quick recovery. You'd never know it happened."

"Dogs are like that."

"I hope you eat steak," I said. "If not, we have salad and grilled veggies."

"I indulge in a steak now and then."

"Great. I just took the meat off the grill to rest. Would you like a tour of the house?"

"I'd love to see it."

I showed her through the rooms, and she made polite comments until we reached my study.

"Wow, that's quite a view you've got from your desk. I imagine it's very inspirational when you're writing."

The window over my computer has a view of the Mississippi winding around the bluffs towards Grafton.

"It is. Before I bought this house, I used to write in the library at Lewis and Clark, but there's no need now. I like to write here."

Jonah had been tagging along and nudged her hand for a stroke.

"You know," she began, "in the scriptures, Jonah has a special calling on him, but is too afraid to do what God asks, so he runs away and hides. Is that why you named him Jonah — because of his struggle with fear?"

"They had already named him at the shelter I adopted him from, possibly for just that reason. He was already used to it and it seemed to suit him. Are you hungry?"

"Famished."

We fixed plates in the kitchen and I poured iced tea from an ancient yellow crock pitcher.

"Is that an antique?" she asked.

"It was my mother's. It's one of the few keepsakes I have of hers. She brewed iced tea from fresh grounds and served it cold and sweet from this pitcher when I was a kid. It takes me back to carefree summer days."

We carried our plates out to a small marble table that overlooks the River Road, and I stashed the sangria on a side bar under a shade tree. There was a soft breeze blowing and the sun was beginning its descent over the river – a perfect evening and good company. The steak was just right – tender and pink in the middle, and the veggies had a nice smoky flavor. We ate with relish for a few moments.

"I was not as close to my mother as I would have liked," I told her, "but it's funny how patterns repeat, isn't it? That's something we focused on in my master's program. My mother was rejected by the boy she loved in high school and married my father – an older man, as soon as she graduated. She got pregnant with Rachael right away, and my life followed the exact same pattern. Were you close with your mother, Jewel?"

"Yes, I was. She found me abandoned as a young girl on the military base and took me in. No one knows how I came to be there and I have no memory of anything before that day, except that my name was Jewel. She and her husband legally adopted me. She was unable to have children and I think I cured her loneliness. She died of cancer when I was twenty."

"Oh, I'm sorry. What was she like?"

"She was rather fragile, and I think the military life was difficult for her, but she loved my father deeply and never regretted her choice. My grandmother, however, never forgave him for 'ruining my mother's chances,' as she put it. My mother came from a wealthy European family and was a classical dancer when my father met her in Paris. She gave up her dream of becoming a prima ballerina to follow him around the world and contented herself with our little family. My grandmother left her considerable wealth in a trust for me and made me promise not to sacrifice my dreams for those of a man." She paused for a moment. "I never did and her money has given me the freedom to travel and do whatever I wanted in life."

"Did you ever meet a man who tempted you to settle down?"

"Yes. David Vaughn." She gave me a rueful smile. "I met him in Europe where we were both involved in a graduate student exchange program, and there was instant, powerful chemistry between us. It frightened me a little bit. I envisioned myself losing touch with my own desires to follow his instead, just as my mother had. He asked me to marry him, but I wasn't sure I could settle for being stuck in remote areas while he dug for buried treasure. I told him I wasn't sure if I ever wanted to get married and accepted a position as a research assistant at Oxford."

She stared at the ground for a moment, then continued. "I think I broke his heart. When he met Cassandra, he was an easy target for her feminine wiles. She got pregnant with Angelique, which I believe she did on purpose, and so he married her. David was considered quite a catch, but he was dedicated to his work and she quelled her loneliness with affairs. It was a shame. I've never met another man who affected me like David."

"I think it's time for that sangria," I told her and headed over to the side bar to retrieve it. I brought it back and poured us both a glass. "To overcoming regrets," I toasted and clinked her glass before we both took a sip.

"What do you regret, Ruby?"

"Not being able to keep my marriage together for the sake of my son. I cared deeply for Chase but there were just too many problems in that marriage to overcome. We both came from broken homes and carried some baggage into that relationship." I didn't feel the need to go into specifics. "I was definitely too young to get married."

"We can't go back and change the past."

"No, we can't. And regret is a good teacher but not a good friend, so it's best to send him packing eventually. That's from the Book of Ruby," I smiled at her.

We sipped our drinks in silence for a moment.

"I imagine your mother's marriage was not easy for her," she said.

"No, it wasn't. She escaped by working part-time at the desk at the Ruebel Hotel in Grafton, right up the street from our house."

"The Ruebel Hotel," she said thoughtfully. "David used to stay there sometimes when he was working the dig in Kampsville and was too tired to drive back to St. Louis. Did he tell you that?"

"No. We talked about Grafton, but I don't believe that ever came up."

"What else did you talk about?" She was smiling at me mysteriously and I didn't say anything right away.

"He told you about the necklace, didn't he?" she asked. "The ruby that was rumored to be buried somewhere in Marib."

"Yes. An old woman in Cairo told him about it. She claimed that very few people knew about the legend, but that Solomon had supposedly given it to Sheba as a parting gift when she returned to her kingdom in the desert. She said part of the legend was that the stone might hold some special power."

"You included the ruby in your novel, but left its power shrouded in mystery," she pointed out.

"I thought it best that way. It added an interesting supernatural element to the story. Such elements are very popular these days and help to sell a book or a movie."

"Do you believe the ruby exists?"

I shrugged. "Do you?"

"David did. He tended to share the legend with any woman he got close to. He was a romantic. It was part of his charm."

The strange smile again. An alarm was starting to sound somewhere inside me, but I held my tongue and waited.

"Did your mother ever tell you why she named you Ruby?"

There was a dull ache forming in the back of my head.

"She said it was an old family name from my father's side..." I trailed off as my head started to pound in earnest and Jewel reached out to grasp my wrist, just as Sophia had, and then she spoke the same words that Sophia had.

"Did David not tell you, Ruby? Did Sophia, before she died? Look inside yourself for the truth."

"I'm not feeling well."

I pulled my wrist free and stood up abruptly, knocking the glass pitcher off the table. It broke into several large pieces and I bent down to pick them up. Jewel squatted down next to me.

"I have to clean this up," I said stupidly.

"No, I'll get it later. Sit down and rest. Drink your sangria."

She eased me back into my chair and I sipped the drink she handed me. My head started to settle down and I became aware of cicadas singing in the night air. Jewel sat down across from me, letting the song of the insects fill the void between us.

"I think I knew it," I finally said. "He never told me, but I think on some level, I knew it."

"He didn't tell you because he only found out shortly before he died. He figured it out when the two of you started talking. Your name, your birthplace and age, your eventual revelation of who your mother was – the pieces fell into place. He met your mother at the Ruebel Hotel and had a brief relationship with her. He didn't know she was married. She wasn't wearing a ring and she didn't tell him. When someone else told him, he broke it off. I mentioned that you have the same coloring as your mother, but David had the same hair color and eyes, and you bear a strong resemblance to him. He noticed that, as well."

"Why did you not tell me right away, when I first saw you again?"

"It's not the sort of thing you just blurt out. And I wasn't sure if you already knew or not. But I was certain that others knew and I came back here to be close to you, in case you needed me."

"Others? Angelique?"

She nodded. "Cassandra overheard David arguing on the phone with your mother. He tracked her down and called to ask her for the truth of it. He told me she finally admitted it to him."

So many pieces were falling into place.

"Rachael said my mother and stepfather were arguing about some man from her past the night they were killed. Maybe that's why he was distracted enough to run off the road." I looked at Jewel. "Did David tell Angelique?"

"No, he told me, and Sophia, but I'm certain he wouldn't have told Angelique. I imagine Cassandra told her, probably out of fear that you would find out about the necklace and lay claim to it. Angelique believes the legend of the necklace is a silly myth, but Cassandra believes it is real and wants it for herself. And your book stirred things up. David had obviously told you about the necklace. I think she believes David had either found it or knew where to look for it, and that maybe he told you."

"If that were the case, why would I have incorporated it into my novel? That would be asking for trouble."

"Yes, but Cassandra is a greedy woman and greed blinds people to reason."

Yes, and someone had searched my house, most likely for the necklace.

"My mother. She never told me."

"Well, perhaps she was going to after she spoke with David but, just like him, she never got the chance. I suspect your mother was as hurt by rejection as you once were. I believe she had strong feelings for David. Perhaps she even hoped he would rescue her from an unhappy marriage. That's probably why she hustled you away from me. She knew David and I were friends. Perhaps she worried I would notice your resemblance to him and mention it to him."

"Why are you telling me now?" I asked her.

"Sophia believed David was abducted and eventually killed because of the necklace. I think she may have been right. I wanted you to be prepared in case you're in danger."

I thought about the dream that had been warning me about another woman in danger. I had buried that ability a long time ago, but perhaps connecting with my real father had triggered something inside me.

I sat in the stillness of the evening with Jewel, absorbing the revelations of the night. It's funny how you can see the truth about others so clearly but hide from the truth about yourself. Angelique was right. It's important to know who you are, and now I did.

I thought about the upcoming cocktail party. I was even less sure that it was a good idea to attend, but sometimes you can't know the consequences until you step into the lion's den.

*****

Chapter 13

As Nicole and I took the steep drive up a private road to the party, the trepidation I felt towards the house was still there, but it was overshadowed by something stronger – that adrenaline rush you feel when something unexpected happens, something potentially dangerous where your wits and skills will be tested in extraordinary circumstances.

Nicole parked her Lincoln Navigator among expensive, mostly foreign vehicles. Her father had instilled in her a dedication to buying American-made cars. He had driven Fords his entire life, and Lincoln, of course, is a division of Ford – Nicole's concession to him. He had lectured me sternly for purchasing a Jaguar. I listened to his lecture out of long-term respect, gave my opinion politely, reminding him that Jaguar had once been owned by Ford, and then took pleasure in the drive home in my Jag, full throttle down the deserted River Road.

We walked to the front door along a flower-lined stone path. Nicole was wearing a turquoise dress that matched her eyes and fell to her knees in feminine layers, silver jewelry and dainty silver sandals. She has the prettiest feet I've ever seen and she played them up with a turquoise gel pedicure.

I was wearing a classic sheath dress in bright yellow, that skimmed my body nicely and showed a decent amount of cleavage – might as well bait the hook. I complemented it with gold jewelry, flat gold sandals, and a nice scent from Estee Lauder's *Pleasures* collection.

"What are you not telling me, Rube?"

"Just be on guard. Some of these people strike me as major players."

I wasn't worried about Nicole. She has good instincts and I knew from experience that the pretty clutch she carried most likely contained a compact 380 caliber Smith and Wesson. She was a Marine's daughter and she had been a Marine's wife, and she was a strong woman in her own right.

She searched my eyes, not completely satisfied, but the front door opened to a dark-haired man who had a street thug look to him, albeit a thug in expensive clothes. He greeted us with a nod, but no smile.

"Good evening, ladies. Come right this way." He spoke with a heavier Spanish accent than Ramirez.

We followed him down a hallway to a great room, which featured the two-story windows visible from below. It was a masculine room with oak paneling, ceramic flooring and black leather seating. An ornate bar decorated one side of the room, where a good number of guests were already mingling.

"Can I get you ladies a drink?"

"Bourbon on the rocks. Sweet Lucy, if you've got it," Nicole gave her standard order.

I gave mine. "Tanqueray and tonic."

He left to get the drinks and Nicole looked at me quizzically. "Who is that guy?"

"Hired help?" I ventured.

"Since when does the hired help wear Armani?"

I shrugged and glanced around the room. I didn't see Ramirez or Angelique yet, but the party had spilled out onto the patio, as well.

"Ah geez, it's Sally Hoyt," Nicole rolled her eyes in disgust. "And here she comes. Where is that guy with my bourbon?"

I braced myself, as well. Sally Hoyt had inherited the La Vista-based general contracting firm founded by her father. She had a reputation as a rude, narcissistic bully who hadn't studied construction in college or worked her way up in the company, like Jamie Sinclair. Instead, she used the firm's assets to make donations to high profile organizations. In return, they let her hold a seat on their board, or speak at seminars on how to become a successful woman CEO in male-dominated industries – an industry insider joke.

"Nicole, I wasn't expecting to see you here! Don't you look nice! And how is that little theater project coming along?"

"That little theater is practically building itself," Nicole said. "Oh, I take that back. Sinclair Construction is building it."

Oh, she was bad. Hoyt Contracting had submitted a bid on the Paramount, and lost out to Sinclair. Sally had requested to see the final numbers, but since it was a privately-owned project, we had exercised our right to deny her request.

The smile faded off her face and her chest turned bright red as she shifted gears and turned her attention to me.

"And Ruby, our famous local author. I think it's so important what you're trying to do for women with your books."

"I'm glad you think so."

My agent had drummed into me the necessity of being cordial to anyone who mentions my books, after he heard me light into an overly zealous critic at a New York book signing.

"Here are your drinks, ladies."

The well-dressed thug was back, but as soon as he handed over our drinks, he bowed politely and disappeared into the crowd.

"Nicole, there's someone I'd like you to meet," Sally tried again. "The developer who is putting together that new women's clinic is here. I don't believe she has an architect yet. Let's go over and chat her up." She put a hand on Nicole's arm, then seemed to remember me at the last minute. "Ruby, would you like to come along?"

"Thank you, no. I would just be in the way, and there's someone else I want to find. You two go ahead."

"Great! See you later, then."

She steered Nicole towards a corner, but not before I caught the *'You're going to pay for this!'* look in Nicole's eyes.

I shrugged my shoulders in apology and took a moment to scan the room again. I was finally standing in the house that was haunting my dreams. I stepped back against a wall and tuned out the noise and the people. It just looked like a well-designed contemporary house, not something frightening. I tried concentrating on the sensations from the dream, but I was not picking up any kind of threatening vibe from the house or anyone in it.

I drifted towards the patio, where faint strains of jazz drifted in from a quartet playing at the edge of the landscaping, interspersed with people talking, laughter, glass clinking. The air held occasional bursts of expensive perfumes and colognes. I passed through the door onto the patio. It was warm out, but not oppressively so, as I wandered through the crowd, sipping my drink and nodding to an occasional acquaintance.

I spotted Ramirez in conversation with two women who looked enraptured by whatever he was saying. His eyes caught mine and he gave me that devastating smile again. It was a good smile – slow, genuine, conveying pleasure, and I felt myself responding to it, as any warm-blooded woman would. He excused himself and made his way towards me. I watched him walk, all animal grace and stylish clothing.

"What do you think?" he gestured broadly.

"The house is just as beautiful as I imagined, what I've seen of it."

"I've been looking forward to seeing you again, Ruby. Let's step over here, out of the traffic."

He took my arm and steered me to a secluded corner. We took a seat on a bench surrounded by potted red geraniums.

"How long do you plan to stay here?" I asked.

"I'm not certain yet. I have commercial investments in several major cities, but Angelique was familiar with this area and thought I might expand the character of my portfolio. Grafton seems to be maxed out, but she's inquiring into some interesting prospects in La Vista. I like the fact that Abraham Lincoln debated Stephen Douglas in the downtown square, and that the city was a stop on the underground railroad for slaves escaping the

South. That gives the area a nice historical flavor on top of the scenic and recreational aspects. There is great potential there."

"Yes," I agreed. "La Vista is well situated on the river between a metropolis like St. Louis and a tourist town like Grafton. The downtown area is connected to the popular River Road, and a short drive from Lambert Airport across the Clark Bridge." The Clark Bridge is an impressive four-lane cable-stay structure that replaced the original two-lane bridge after the Great Flood. "Have you seen it lit up at night? It's beautiful."

"No, I've not had the pleasure. I understand you are a partner in the theater rehab that is underway. How did you go from writing to commercial development?"

"I worked for an architect who was a major developer in downtown St. Louis while I was earning my master's degree, and my best friend is an architect. We are both dedicated to furthering the redevelopment of La Vista. I grew up in this area and La Vista is where I raised my son, so it's close to my heart. Where did you grow up?"

"Phoenix. We were very poor. My father abandoned my mother when she got pregnant with me, and she worked as a housekeeper at the Phoenician to support us."

"I used to visit a cousin in Phoenix," I told him. "This was before I had money too, and he and I pretended to be guests and sneaked into the Phoenician's swimming pool once. What I remember is the great view of Camelback Mountain and the swim-up margarita bar."

"Yes, I worked at that bar for a time," he said. "Perhaps I made you a drink. I make a mean margarita!"

His smile was truly beautiful. And his eyelashes were ridiculously long, which only served to enhance his dark eyes. I was trying not to like him but he had a very strong charisma, and I had to remind myself of the incident at Aeries.

"How did *you* get interested in commercial development?" I asked him.

"Oh, I determined early on that I was not going to be poor all of my life. I attended the University of Arizona, made connections at my job, and picked up valuable bits of information from rich patrons who were full of tequila and liked to brag to a harmless bartender." He winked at me.

"Hello, Ruby. I'm glad you were able to make it."

I'd been engrossed in the conversation and hadn't seen Angelique approach. She looked fit and tan in a white halter dress. She wore her hair loose, and a silver band studded with jade on her upper arm. Ramirez stood up and so did I.

"I told you I wouldn't miss it," I answered.

"Rey, the contractor I wanted you to meet is here," she told him. "I thought he could tell you about the project we looked at yesterday. He's very knowledgeable."

"Of course. I'm going to freshen my drink first. Can I get you ladies anything?"

"No, I'm good. Ruby?"

"Fine here." I waved my glass. I was pacing myself on alcohol.

He gave us a little bow and headed across the patio, and Angelique turned her attention to me. It was so strange to think she was my half-sister. All those years when I never knew she existed. But I was determined to proceed with caution.

"Rey seems quite taken with you." She was clearly not pleased by that.

"He's a good conversationalist and we have a mutual interest. Are you involved with him personally?"

"To some degree," she shrugged noncommittally and nodded her head towards Jamie and his wife across the patio, talking with a Grafton alderman. "Is that his wife?"

This was said with an incredulous tone of voice. Elizabeth Hayden had possessed the right social background but she was not what you'd call a looker, with her short, curly brown hair, thin figure and slight overbite. I had met her on several occasions. She had a friendly personality and a good sense of style. Designer clothes can't completely compensate for a lack of beauty, but she had other qualities to bring to a marriage, including a stable, socially connected family.

"Yes, that's Liz Sinclair."

She gave me a questioning look.

"They have a daughter and Jamie loves her very much," I said, then realized I sounded defensive, and it was really none of Angelique's business.

"Daughters can be very precious to their fathers." She looked at me pointedly.

I wasn't going to take the bait. I saw Ramirez approaching and used that opportunity. "Here comes Rey. I'll leave you to your business. I'm going to mingle."

I stepped neatly around her back and escaped through the crowd, heading back towards the great room. On the way, I spotted Cassandra Vaughn in conversation with someone I didn't know. Her stare was just as frigid as the first time. I ignored her and made my way back inside. I wandered across the room, and saw Nicole still deep in conversation with Sally and the developer. I hoped she'd land a project for her trouble.

I took another good look at the room with its cathedral ceiling and expensive artwork. When my eyes landed on an arched doorway in the back corner my vision suddenly blurred, then I saw the vivid image of a heavy oak door, before it faded away. The sounds in the room felt like they were coming from a long distance. The doorway beckoned to me and I felt a sense of dread that was impossible to ignore as I drifted towards it.

I dropped my glass off on the bar and took a quick look around. No one was paying me any attention and I continued to move forward. I passed through the doorway and followed a long hallway that curved around to the right. I was moving on pure instinct. It was like one of those old haunted mansion movies where someone is being pulled irresistibly down a darkened hallway towards something sinister and you wonder why they don't just turn around and run. But there was something back there I needed to see and I realized it was behind the oak door.

The deeper into the hallway I traveled, the stronger the sense of dread closed in around me. I followed one last curve and spotted it at the end of the hall. Only a few dim sconces lit the way and I moved forward in acute fear. I expected it to be locked, but when I tried the knob the door swung open into a room made even darker by the fact that it had no windows. I could make out a big brass bed in front of me, and the outline of a bedside table with a lamp.

As I stood in the middle of that room, I was filled with a fear so strong I could almost taste it. The room reverberated with something dark and forbidden. I jumped when I heard a noise down the hall and made my way back to the door, slipped into the empty hallway and closed the door behind me. A man stepped out of the shadows, startling me, and I struggled to compose myself.

"Can I help you find something?" he asked.

It was the Hispanic guy who'd answered the door and the tone of his voice and the look on his face were openly hostile. Up close, I could see it was a combination of the sharp planes of his face, small, close-set eyes and slicked-back hair that gave him the street thug appearance.

"There you are," called a male voice. "I've been waiting down the hall for you. You must have taken a wrong turn."

I recognized Derek Jericho moving towards me from the opposite hallway. He gave me a suggestive grin and pulled me against him in a familiar manner. Before I could react, he turned to the other man and the look on his face turned decidedly feral.

"You'll have to find your own date, Ramirez. This woman is spoken for."

The man looked us over for a moment, then gave a curt nod.

"No harm intended, Jericho. I thought the lady was lost. It's easy to do in this house. Perhaps you would be wise to return to the party."

"Yeah, we'll do that," Jericho said. "It's obvious there's no privacy to be found back here."

The Hispanic guy turned and walked briskly away and I became aware that I was grasping Jericho's arms and my body was still pressed against his. It was a solid, muscular body underneath another crisp white shirt, and I looked up into his face and got my first real life close-up. He was handsome. Not in a pretty boy way like Rey Ramirez, but ruggedly masculine. There was a faint scar on his left cheek that only added to his manly aura. The green eyes were fixed on my face and he looked concerned.

"What were you thinking, snooping around back here? What were you looking for?"

I liked his voice. It was just as masculine as the rest of him, with a barely detectable British accent.

"You called him Ramirez," I said.

"Yeah. That's Rey's cousin Marco — his right-hand man. And he's not someone you should be alone with in a dark hallway."

I hadn't been with a man in a long time and the proximity of his body was distracting me. I forced myself to focus.

"I didn't come back here unprotected."

At his questioning look, I lifted my dress and nodded towards my thigh, where my dagger was strapped down in a sheath. His eyes came back up to mine with what looked like admiration, for the dagger or the thigh, or perhaps a little of both. When he reached down and pulled the dagger free to get a better look, my breath caught in surprise and my heart started to beat a little faster. I do like an assertive guy.

"Nice blade. Nice ruby too," he said, admiring the jewel embedded in the hilt.

"My former husband introduced me to knives on camping trips. I used part of my first book advance to have this dagger made. It makes me feel safer in secluded locations."

"That's a smart move, but do you think you could use it on someone like Ramirez?"

"I promise you'll be the first to know if I do." I stuck it back in the sheath and straightened my dress. "What are *you* doing back here?"

"Following Ramirez, who was obviously following *you*. He followed you to the soccer game yesterday too."

I remembered the glimpse of a dark-haired man in the trees, who seemed to be watching me.

"Why were you following him?"

"I had my private investigator following him because I believe he was involved in the disappearance of my fiancée, Melanie Mayhall. I just haven't been able to prove it yet." He pulled my card out of his pants pocket. "You apparently made a detour on your way home. Something I can do for you?"

I searched his eyes for a long moment, trying to decide how to answer that. "I think we should talk, but not here."

"Agreed."

He pulled out his wallet and produced a card of his own. The graphic on his card was of a stately building with a blue background. It read *Derek Jericho, Blue London* with a cell number and email address. Since I wasn't carrying a purse, I tucked it into my bodice, trying to ignore the seductive smile on his face.

"We should get back out there, before we draw any more attention," he said as he took my hand and pulled me down the hall.

I glanced over my shoulder at the oak door, relieved to be leaving it behind, but troubled that I was even more in the dark than before.

"I'll pick you up for lunch tomorrow," he said as we passed through the archway.

"I'll text you my address."

"I know where you live."

He dropped my hand as we reached the bar.

"Two Tanqueray and tonics," he told the bartender.

He seemed to know a lot about me. I scanned the room and my heart skipped a beat when I spotted Nicole in conversation with Rey and Angelique. Apparently, so did Jericho.

"Let's go head that off at the pass," he said as he handed me my drink and put a hand to the small of my back to propel me forward.

Nicole was saying something about the theater project as we approached. Ramirez had been listening intently, but turned to smile at me. Angelique seemed more interested in Jericho. She looked at him with what appeared to be a mixture of anger and desire. I wondered about their history.

"Ramirez, as usual, you're surrounded by beautiful women," Jericho said. "If you could bottle that charm, you could retire and disappear into the jungle somewhere. We'd all be heartbroken, of course."

"I don't remember inviting you, Jericho. Angelique must have remedied that for me."

"Angie and I go way back," he said, then extended his hand to Nicole. "Derek Jericho, Ms. Gordon. It's a pleasure to meet you in person. I'm an admirer of your work."

Nicole shook his hand and looked at me questioningly, trying to gauge the dynamics. "Isn't that interesting? Apparently, so is Mr. Ramirez. A girl can't have too many admirers. But we're talking architecture, right?"

"Yes," Angelique stepped in. "We're aware that Nicole has done some rehab work with Sinclair Construction and thought we might team up for a project. We're looking at some prospects in downtown La Vista. She's agreed to meet us tomorrow to have a look at one."

I looked at Nicole, trying to hide my alarm.

"I'm aware that one of the properties we're looking at is of interest to you, Ruby; or rather, to Broadway Comeback," Angelique continued. "That's the name of your joint venture with Nicole, correct? You're interested in the old Stratton Hotel, right?" She turned to Jericho. "Some people believe that was the hotel used by certain famous St. Louis sex researchers for their clandestine affair. Isn't *that* interesting? It's lain abandoned for decades."

He raised his eyebrows and nodded, appearing only half-interested as he grabbed a shrimp wrapped in bacon from a passing waiter.

"Unfortunately," she went on, turning back to me, "I've already submitted a bid on that property, on behalf of Rey. I'm waiting to hear back from the realtor to see if it was accepted."

"I can spare you the wait," Jericho cut in. "I closed on that property two days ago, on behalf of Broadway Comeback. I was also aware of Ruby's interest in it. I'm just a silent partner. Mmmm, I just love these bacon-wrapped shrimp, Angie."

He took my glass and set both of our drinks on a passing tray, wiping his hands on the waiter's towel, as Nicole and I struggled to keep our faces impassive, upon hearing his surprising revelation.

"Unfortunately, Ruby and Nicole need to be going now," he said. "I'll walk them out. Great party, Ramirez. Angie, always a pleasure."

He put one hand on my back and one on Nicole's and steered us towards the door.

"Good night," I called over my shoulder.

"We'll see you tomorrow, Nicole," Angelique called after her, and Nic shot a little wave their way. Angie looked none too pleased, but it was the look on Ramirez's face that worried me - deadly cold and silent.

Marco Ramirez met us in the foyer and the look on his face as he opened the door was equally hostile.

"Be careful out there, Jericho. It's a big, dangerous world."

"Oh, I'm a very cautious fellow, Ramirez. You should know that by now."

"This guy is a keeper," Nicole whispered to me as we stepped outside.

"What are your plans with them tomorrow, Nicole?" he asked as we reached her car.

"Well, I'm going to meet them at the Wedge Building. It's an older-style office building that's on the market for a good price. They mentioned something about having lunch. What is this about your buying the Stratton for Broadway Comeback?"

"I'm having lunch with Ruby tomorrow. I'll fill her in then. You be careful what you reveal to those two. I've known them for a long time. I'd advise you against doing any business with Ramirez."

"I'll keep that in mind. And I look forward to seeing you again."

"Same here," he smiled at her as she got behind the wheel.

He opened the door for me. "I'll pick you up at 11:00. Let's get an early start."

"Okay."

He closed the door and I ignored the smirk on Nicole's face as she fired the engine and started down the drive.

"Aren't you full of surprises," she said.

So was Jericho, apparently. I wondered what his interest in me entailed. Sophia had thought it important that I find him. I decided it was time to fill Nicole in on some things. She knew about my interviews with David and about his disappearance and death. I told her he had apparently been my natural father and that Jewel Alexander had divulged that to me, and that I believed Sophia had been in the process of telling me when she died. She looked at me in concern.

"Are you okay?"

"Yes, I'm fine. I'm just sorry I never got the chance to meet my real father in person."

"That makes Angelique your half-sister. Have you talked to her about it?"

"No. And I don't plan to until I get a better handle on the situation, so don't tell her anything."

I told her that I suspected the lot of them were searching for the ruby necklace and might believe I could lead them to it.

"It's possible they might think you know something about it too, since we're so close," I told her.

"I'll see if I can find out what they want, but I won't commit to working with them," she assured me.

I hesitated for a moment, then followed my instincts.

"Nicole, be careful around Rey. I don't trust him. And I'm not sure I trust Angelique yet either."

I thought about the series of events at Aeries, when Sophia had died. I still wasn't sure of exactly what I had seen or how that had transpired. I told Nicole I'd been having some dreams lately, like the ones I'd had when we were kids, and that I had dreamed there was something dangerous about Ramirez. She took me seriously.

"What about Derek? He has some history with them. Do you trust *him*?" she asked.

"I think so. But he's full of surprises too, so I'm being cautious."

"Did he really buy the Stratton for us to work on together?"

"I guess," I answered. "But how he knew we wanted it, I have no idea. I do know that money does not seem to be a problem for him. He owns a successful venture capital firm. Are you familiar with Blue London?"

"I thought his name sounded familiar," Nicole nodded. "Well, he's loaded then. Although I think historically they've been more involved in startups than real estate, at least in St. Louis, but that company has a stellar reputation."

"I'll see what else I can find out tomorrow," I said.

"Me too. And don't worry, I'll be careful."

Nicole dropped me at home and I went to bed early, emotionally exhausted by the evening's events. I fell into a fitful sleep, haunted by the oak door and the raw fear that had enveloped me.

"Ruby..."

I opened my eyes. The room was dark. Jonah slept peacefully at the foot of my bed.

"Ruby..." I heard it again. Faint, feminine.

I reached behind the nightstand and pulled out my Beretta, releasing the safety. I moved cautiously across the room and checked the hall. It was empty. I glanced back at Jonah. He lifted his head to see what I was doing, then settled back into sleep, apparently satisfied there was no threat.

I was not. I felt drawn to the window at the end of the hall and moved towards it slowly, my heart pounding. When I reached it, I moved to the side of it, out of sight, and glanced tentatively through the edge of the glass... and caught my breath in surprise. Angelique stood on my lawn, past the pool area, still wearing the white halter dress. She was looking up at the window, like she expected to see me there.

I moved quickly down the stairs, looking all around, but I didn't believe anyone was in the house. I took a moment to glance out a side window to check the drive. There were no cars there, and I disarmed the alarm and continued out the patio doors to an empty lawn. She was nowhere in sight.

I ran to the spot where I'd seen her and looked all around. In frustration, I turned back to the house and looked up in disbelief. She was standing in the same window I'd seen her from, looking down at me.

I ran back inside and all the way up the stairs. She was not at the window and I ran breathlessly down the hall to my bedroom. Jonah was still sleeping peacefully on my bed. I stepped into the hall and called out to her.

"Angelique! Come out and face me!"

Jonah awoke with a start and looked at me like I'd lost it.

"Angelique!"

Jonah slipped out of bed and followed me curiously as I did a systematic check of the house, just as I had when someone had searched it. I found no one, and no evidence that anyone had been inside. I reset the alarm, made myself a stiff gin and tonic and drank it straight down, hoping it would help me sleep.

I crawled back into bed, and put the gun back into its hiding place. Jonah fell back into an easy sleep, but I did not. I was hyper alert to the smallest sounds in the house. All the fear that I had felt as a child when the visions started was descending on me. I finally calmed myself by focusing on a certain green-eyed man and eventually followed his image into a deep, dreamless sleep.

*****

Peggy Estes

Chapter 14

I was wandering the grounds, ruminating about Angelique's appearance, when Jericho arrived. Jonah ran up to meet him and he bent to wrestle with him for a moment. Jonah liked him. That was a good sign, as Jonah did not generally take to men immediately, except for Max, but all dogs love Max.

I watched him walk towards me with Jonah trailing at his heels. He was wearing jeans, loafers with no socks, and a royal blue shirt with the sleeves rolled back that looked great with his coloring. My heart skipped a beat and I felt a little ridiculous. I couldn't remember any man affecting me in quite that way.

"How are you this morning?" he asked.

"Great, thank you. I see you've met Jonah."

"Yes. He seems like a good dog."

Jonah sensed we were talking about him and gave his signature pounce towards Jericho, then sprinted towards the trees, hoping Derek would give chase. He only laughed and turned back to me.

"This is a nice house. How do you like it here?"

"I like it a lot. Living on the bluffs above the River Road feels right to me. How did you know where I live, by the way?"

"I hope you'll forgive me, but I ran a background check on you. A man like me learns to gather intel on all the players in the game."

I tried to decide which reference to pursue – a man like him or the players in the game.

"A man like you?"

"Yes. Since I took the liberty of checking into your background, I'll return the favor for you. I'm ex special forces – a Navy Seal, to be precise. After I left the military, I joined my father's venture capital firm – something I fought against when I was growing up. But it suits me. I like the risk and the sense of independence. After he died, I concentrated on our St. Louis office to be closer to my mother. She lives in Ladue, which is where I grew up and went to school. I'm her only child. My parents divorced when I was young and my father moved back to London, where my mother had met him, and based himself out of the firm's original office. I spent my summers there with him. And now you know all the news worth knowing."

"Not all the news."

I had strolled over to a bench and took a seat. I gestured to the spot next to me and he sat down.

"I'm sorry to be so bold, but since we're laying the cards out on the table here, will you tell me about your fiancée?"

A shadow crossed his face and I tamped down the little stab of jealousy that elicited.

"I met Mel when we both attended Wash U," he began. "I studied economics and she was an archaeology major. I kept it casual because I knew I was going to enlist after college. It was something I just needed to do. We kept in touch during those years, but sporadically, because I was off on classified missions much of the time. We eventually lost touch, but reconnected by coincidence." He paused to smile at me, then continued. "The foundation for the archaeologists working in Marib invited me to a fundraising lunch at Wash U. Melanie was there with David Vaughn. She was working closely with him, as his research assistant. I made a contribution to the dig, and Mel and I picked up where we had left off. Eventually, I asked her to marry me."

"But she disappeared, shortly before David?"

"Yes, while she was visiting him in Marib and doing some research in Cairo. She split her time between there and St. Louis. She knew about his interest in the ruby necklace, or rather, the legend of the necklace. Sophia believed that's why David was taken, and probably why Mel was also taken."

"But, unlike David, she's never been found?" I asked.

"No. But I haven't given up on finding her."

"You said you believe Marco Ramirez was involved. Do you believe the Ramirez men are looking for the necklace then?"

"Yes. But I don't believe that's the only reason why they took Melanie."

"Why, then?"

He drew a ragged breath and I could see the toll it was taking on him to tell me about this.

"I believe they're dealing in the white slave trade — selling beautiful white women to men in places where they are a rare commodity."

I sat in shocked silence for a moment. "Do you have any proof?" I finally asked.

"I don't have hard evidence, but I know in my gut that's what happened. Melanie told me she had met Rey through Angelique when he came to tour the dig and to make a contribution. She told me that he made her feel uncomfortable. When she disappeared, I looked deeper into his background. He was once investigated for transporting stolen goods over intercontinental lines, but no charges were filed. And he's been involved in some business dealings with people who are suspected of being connected to the sex trade. Those deals were legitimate on face, but I still suspect he was involved with their illegal dealings behind the scene."

I thought about that whole scenario for a moment.

"If that's the case, why haven't they sold Angelique?" I asked. "She's very beautiful."

"Yes, but she's more valuable to them as a legitimate business front."

That made sense.

"Do you have any leads on Melanie?"

"The initial leads did not pan out and the case went cold. The authorities have stopped investigating. It's common for people to disappear in Yemen and the number of missing women is astronomical. Human trafficking is widespread, with connections to neighboring Gulf countries. It's easy to make a woman disappear there. When Ramirez came to this area, I started inquiring into his dealings again to see if I could learn anything new."

"I'm so sorry."

I reached out instinctively to rub his shoulder and he turned to search my eyes. I found myself fighting to focus again.

"You said you and Angelique go way back. How did you meet her? Through Melanie and David?"

He looked uncomfortable for just a second.

"No. I met her at Wash U, as well. She was pre-law then and she pursued me, very aggressively.

We went out a few times, but she was not my type. We reconnected through Mel and David. She was representing Ramirez by that time, and that's how I became familiar with him. This isn't the first time he and I have competed for a project. I chalk that up to Angelique trying to insinuate herself back into my life. She doesn't like to take no for an answer."

"No, I can see that about her," I said. "Which reminds me, I really don't like Nicole being alone with them. Shall we head into town?"

"Absolutely."

I put Jonah back inside, grabbed my purse and met him in the driveway. He steered me to a black Audi A8 and opened the passenger door for me. I thought it suited him – all raw masculine power with a classy exterior.

We chatted about the area until we reached the Stratton. He pulled over across the street from it and we both sat looking at it for a moment.

"Were you serious about buying this for us to develop together?"

He turned back to me with a wicked smile that left Rey Ramirez's in the dust, as far as I was concerned.

"Yes. I think you have good instincts and I like what you've both done with the theater. My sources told me you'd been looking at this property, but didn't have the funds to purchase it yet. They also told me Angelique had made an appointment to see it, so I decided to step in. I like to thwart Ramirez whenever possible, but I also thought it would be fun, and lucrative, to do a project with you. Nicole is a good architect, and this property qualifies for TIF and block grant funds." He squeezed my arm. "I meant what I said about a silent partner. I promise I won't try to drive the project creatively, but you can ask my opinion, whenever you like. And whether you'd like to sell the property when it's finished or retain ownership does not matter to me. We can work out a mutually satisfactory deal either way. My attorney is drawing up an agreement for you to look at. I don't believe your attorney will find anything in it to contest."

I returned his smile, somewhat at a loss. He seemed to be asking nothing in return.

"That's very generous of you. I don't know what to say."

"Just say we have a deal."

He stuck out his hand.

"Okay. If Nicole and our attorney are good with it, we have a deal."

I gripped his hand and felt a jolt of pure physical attraction. I think he felt it too, from the way he was looking at me. My mouth turned dry and I realized I was still holding his hand.

"I'm suddenly very thirsty. Did you have someplace in mind?" I asked.

He smiled and started the engine. "Do you have a favorite spot around here?"

"I do. Jimmy the Greek's. It's a wonderful little hole in the wall place further down the Broadway corridor."

I directed him back down Broadway, where we eventually came upon the Wedge Building. I pointed it out to him and he slowed as we passed it.

"I see where it got its name."

"Yes," I laughed. "It's actually shaped like a wedge. The original developers could only secure a small amount of frontage on Broadway, but they expanded the building out towards the rear. It's become a local landmark. Look, there's Nicole's car. Is that Angelique's Ferrari?"

"It is. Would you like to stop in and surprise them?"

I pulled out my cell and sent Nic a text.

You okay?

Fine. Don't worry, she came right back.

"No," I told him. "She says she's okay. Let's give her some time."

I sent back a reply. *We're close by, if you need us.*

The affable owner greeted us at the door, and a waitress showed us to a counter-height table in the back, with a nice view of the rest of the room. We ordered iced tea and flatbread pizza.

"What else did you learn about me?"

He hesitated a moment, probably deciding which pieces he should share.

"I have a brief sketch of your childhood, your marriage, son and divorce, the deaths in your family, and your education and career."

"So, all the news worth knowing," I repeated.

"Not all the news," he shot right back.

I stopped mid-sip, set my glass down and waited.

"I know that David Vaughn was your real father."

I wasn't expecting that and waited silently for him to continue.

"Melanie knew. David had confided it to her. They were very close. She told no one else but me. She had no secrets from me." He looked at me closely. "You did know this, right? She said David was planning to tell you. I felt certain either he or Sophia would have told you."

"Neither one of them got the chance. It was Jewel Alexander who told me, very recently."

"David's good friend," he nodded. "I knew she was back in the area. I trust her."

"Me too," I agreed.

"I was sorry to hear of Sophia's death. I had business out of town and was unable to make the memorial service, but I liked her. I know that you were with her when she died. I'm sorry. That must have been difficult."

There wasn't much about me he didn't know, and it left me a little off-balance.

"I saw you at her lecture," I blurted out, for lack of a better direction.

"Yes," he grinned. "I saw you too."

I felt my face grow warm. This man made me feel like a young girl again. The pizza arrived and when the waitress left, he politely shifted gears.

"Mel said you interviewed David for your book. I'm sure that's where you got the idea for the necklace in your plot. You do realize that you inadvertently dangled a carrot to these people?"

I shrugged my shoulders. "I can't help what other people infer."

"In any case, they're dangerous, and I intend to be a presence in your life." He looked at me, trying to gauge my reaction. "While they're in the area," he added.

I tried not to feel hurt over that. It was natural. He had a fiancée and was still holding out hope that she was alive and he would find her. I knew from the statistics I had read on that subject that if she had been sold into the sex trade in a foreign country, it wasn't likely he would ever see her again. The longer a woman was gone in that situation, the less likely she would ever be found. I didn't wish that on any woman, or the not knowing on him. I hoped he would find some resolution to the situation.

"May I see a picture of her?" I asked impulsively.

He smiled faintly and pulled out his cell, scrolled through some photos and set it down in front of me. She was standing on a balcony, with her back to a wrought iron fence, smiling at the camera. She was pretty, with long dark hair. I had entertained a sudden suspicion that she might be the woman in trouble in my dream, which would explain why he was in the dream, but it wasn't her.

"She's very pretty," I said, and he nodded and put it back in his pocket. "I hope you find her."

"Thank you."

"Did you also run a check on Nicole?" I thought to ask.

"Of course. She's a potential business partner. But not an extensive check. I know about her husband. A Marine who died in combat in Afghanistan."

"Kyle," I nodded. "He was the love of her life."

"Afghanistan is a dangerous place. I lost some friends there, myself. Nicole strikes me as a smart woman, but I'd feel better if she kept her distance from the Ramirez boys. I don't believe she's in danger of being abducted. Mel was working a low-profile job that required her to spend time in remote areas. She was an easy target. But Nicole has a high-profile career and strong family support. She would be missed, and several people know she's with Ramirez. I believe his interest in her is to see if she knows anything about the necklace. Ramirez has a lot of confidence in his ability to charm women."

I heard his cell phone vibrate quietly from his pants pocket.

"Excuse me," he said and pulled it out to discreetly check a text message. He smiled at me as he tucked it back into his pocket, and we finished eating, then drove back up Broadway. Their cars were gone from the Wedge.

Checking in, I texted Nic.

Lunch at the Café. On my home turf.

Okay. I'll check in later.

We chatted easily on the drive up the River Road. He was a fascinating man and I enjoyed his company very much. When we pulled into my drive, he jumped out and opened the door for me, walked me to the entrance and waited while I disarmed the alarm. I liked his gentlemanly manners.

"Thank you for lunch. I enjoyed being with you."

"I enjoyed being with you, too. I'll call you later tonight."

"Okay."

I impulsively reached up and kissed him on the cheek — something my mother had instilled in me as a child with people I cared about. He looked pleasantly surprised as I slipped inside and closed the door behind me.

I tried to get some work done on my new book, but I couldn't get focused. All I could think about was Derek Jericho. Eventually, I gave up, slipped into the shower and indulged in risqué thoughts about him while the water sluiced over me. Enough said on that.

*****

Chapter 15

I tried a couple of different times to reach Nicole, but got no response. I wasn't going to relax completely until I heard from her. I succumbed to my restlessness and hopped in my car to head back into town. On an impulse, I drove by the Paramount site, slowing to admire the newly restored art deco marquee.

There was a Sinclair truck parked off to the side. It wasn't Jamie's, with his distinctive license plate. I pulled in and tried the front door. It was unlocked.

"Hello?" I called out.

After a moment, I recognized the foreman stepping into the lobby area.

"Oh, hi, Ms. January. Something I can do for you?"

"No thanks, Nate, I was just driving by and was curious to see who was here on a Saturday."

"Oh, don't worry," he laughed. "I'm not on the clock. I just stopped by to pick up some drawings and started tinkering with something. I'm about to clear out. Were you looking for Jamie? You just missed him."

"He was here?"

"Yeah. He met some good-looking blonde here. Picked her up on his Harley. Not sure how that would go over with the missus. She was a real stunner."

This day had started out great, but was taking a bad turn.

"That was probably Angelique. She's a real estate attorney. I didn't see her car outside."

"Yeah, that's what he called her. Someone in a black Ferrari dropped her off."

"Did they say where they were going?"

"No, but it's a beautiful day for a ride."

He had that knowing look on his face that men reserve for one another regarding female conquest.

"Thanks. I won't keep you any longer."

I made my way back to my car and headed for the market. It wasn't like Nicole to ignore my calls. I spotted her car where she normally parks, and heaved a sigh of relief. I parked and went up the private stairs to knock at her studio. She didn't answer, so I went up to the third floor to knock at her loft. I heard Ginger bark, but she didn't answer there either. I went down into the market and spotted June behind the counter.

"Oh hey, sweetie, what brings you in today?" she asked.

"I was looking for Nic. She's not answering the door or her phone. Have you seen her?"

"Have I ever! She left here with some gorgeous dark-haired guy. He looked like a movie star too. There's a real rash of that going around. She didn't say where they were going, but that's okay. I was just glad to see her with an attractive man."

I struggled to keep my alarm from showing. "It's not like her to ignore my calls, but I guess she's distracted."

"Oh, there's a good reason for that." She reached in her apron pocket and pulled out a familiar-looking cell phone. "She forgot her phone. I found it on the table after she left. But hopefully she'll have more on her mind than chatting," she grinned. "I'll tell her you're looking for her, hon."

She stepped away to wait on a customer and I fought a wave of serious panic. I got back into my car once again and headed for the River Road, purely on instinct. I wondered briefly if I should call Derek, but I didn't want to sound hysterical. He had a point about so many people knowing who Nicole was with.

The drive up the River Road seemed to take forever, even with the Jag wide open. I didn't spot the Ferrari or Jamie's distinctive touring class Harley on the drive. As I neared Grafton, I slowed down and, on impulse, pulled into the Wind Rivers Condos. I didn't know which one Angelique was renting, so I drove through slowly looking for a clue, which I didn't find – no Harley, no Ferrari.

I drove through town keeping my eyes peeled, to no avail. I pulled into the parking lot of St. Patrick's, got out and leaned back against my car to look up at the bluff house. Déjà vu.

A blue BMW drove by on the street behind the church – the one that leads past the private drive to the bluff house. It slowed down, backed up and pulled onto the parking lot.

Cassandra Vaughn got out, pulling off a pair of designer sunglasses, and walked towards me. She was dressed in an expensive-looking pair of cream slacks and a matching shell, broken up by a thin gold belt. Her hair was styled in a loose chignon and she carried herself like old money. When she reached me, she turned to look up at the house, then back at me.

"What is your interest in Rey?" she asked baldly.

"How is that any of your business?" I matched her cold tone. As far as I was concerned, the gloves were off with her, too.

She looked me up and down, as if I were an insect she was trying to decide how to dispose of.

"If you think I believe that nasty rumor about your mother and my late husband, you are sadly mistaken. I don't believe for a moment that David would lower himself to dally with townie trash. So, if you're thinking of making any public claims to that effect, I can assure you, my attorneys will issue a cease and desist order and I will expose you for fraud. I don't believe that's the type of press your publicist will appreciate."

For just a moment, I permitted myself to pity my father for being married to such a harpy, but just for a moment, and then I stepped into her personal space.

"I can't imagine what possessed my father to spend time with you, but I know what kept him chained to you. Getting yourself knocked up is the oldest trick in the book, even for well-bred women. I'm glad he got to spend some time with my mother before your life sentence ensnared him. I'm sure he looked back on that experience fondly." I watched the blood drain from her face and spared a glance up at the bluff house. "You appear to be coming from the Ramirez house. What is *your* interest in Rey? Or is it Marco? Or both?"

At this point, she looked like she wanted to choke me. With her emotions on the edge, I went in for the kill.

"You believe that ruby necklace really exists, don't you? And you think my father told me where to find it. If that were the case, do you actually believe I would be stupid enough to advertise it in my novel? You're not the sharpest blade, are you?"

She struggled to regain her composure, then spat out evenly, "I hope there's a special place in Hell for uppity little tarts."

"Be careful what you wish for," I shot back.

She stuck her nose in the air and made her way back to her car, got in and drove off. I turned back to the house and had just made the decision to drive up there when my attention was captured by the red front doors of the church opening. Jewel emerged, smiled at me and sat down on the steps. I tamped down my emotions and strolled over to her.

"I would say we have to stop meeting this way," she said, "but since you're a writer, I'll spare you the cliché."

"I don't mind the occasional well-placed cliché," I said and sat down next to her. "Were you spending some time in contemplation?"

"There's something special about having a sacred space all to yourself," she said, then nodded toward the bluff. "You're back to looking at that house again. That's where Rey Ramirez is staying, isn't it?"

"Yes. And I have a bad feeling my best friend Nicole may be up there with him. I think he's a dangerous man. And so does Derek. He thinks Rey and his cousin Marco are involved in some repulsive business dealings, including the sex trade. He believes that's what happened to his fiancée. Did you know that?"

"I've heard that theory mentioned," she said, "but I don't believe anyone has been able to produce any evidence. Sophia thought she was taken because of the ruby necklace. They're both disturbing prospects. So you've made friends with Jericho, then," she smiled at me. "He's a smart man and very capable." She paused for a moment. "Nicole Gordon. I remember her as a young girl. I used to see her riding a dirt bike on the trail through the woods behind my house. A gutsy girl, to be sure, but I wouldn't like to see her alone with Ramirez either. Are you going up there to check on her?"

"Yes. And I just had a nasty run-in with Cassandra Vaughn. She seemed to be coming from there. Do you think she's involved with Rey in some way?"

"I wouldn't be surprised. She's always had self-serving relationships with men. Would you like me to go up there with you?"

"No, I think it would look odd if I took you up there with me. I went to a cocktail party there last night. That's where Nicole met Rey, so I feel responsible for that. I'll be okay. I'll call you if I need help. Hey, I just realized I don't have your cell number."

"I'll text it to you while you're driving up there. And I'll be close by if you need me," she assured me.

"Okay then."

I went back to my car and drove past her. True to her word, I received a text from an unfamiliar cell number as I parked the car.

This is Jewel, came the message. I stored her in my contacts, stuck my phone in my pocket and glanced around. There was only a van in the driveway – no Ferrari, but it could be in the garage. I made my way to the front and rang the bell.

After a couple of moments, the door opened. I was half-expecting to see Marco but, instead, it was a young woman wearing a polo shirt with a Daisy Maids logo on it.

"Can I help you?" she asked.

"Yes, is Mr. Ramirez home?"

"No, I'm sorry. There's no one here right now. Just my crew and me. We clean this house every week."

"Oh, well you're cleaning up after the party last night then."

"Yes," she rolled her eyes. "Kind of a mess today. Can I give Mr. Ramirez a message for you?"

"Actually, I was here last night for the party and I think I left my cell phone here. Do you mind if I come in and have a look?"

She looked at me uncertainly. "I don't know. Maybe I could look for you."

Another girl appeared behind her and blurted out, "Oh my God! You're Ruby January, aren't you?

You wrote that *Desert Queen* book. My mom and I both loved that book! Can I get your autograph?"

"Sure. Do you have a pen and paper inside?"

"I'll find one. Come on in." She motioned me to follow her down the hall. "I recognized you from your picture on the book cover. I knew you lived somewhere around here. My mom is not going to believe this!"

The other girl shrugged her shoulders and closed the door behind me as I followed the fan girl into the great room. She dug in her purse for a paper and pen while the other girl headed for a room in the back.

"You'd better not take too long, Roberta," she called. "We're behind schedule already. And you'd better not let that Ramirez guy catch you with someone in here," she called over her shoulder before she disappeared from sight.

Roberta rolled her eyes. "She's right on that one. Rey Ramirez is sexy as hell, but his cousin gives me the creeps."

"I know what you mean. He seems like a scary guy. Tell me something. I thought I saw Cassandra Vaughn coming from here on my way up. Was she in the house?"

"You mean that snobby blonde lady?"

I nodded.

"She came to the door looking for Marco. When I told her he wasn't here, she threw a hissy fit. Here you go."

She passed me the paper and pen.

"What's your mother's name?" I asked.

"Darla!"

I scribbled my thanks and best wishes to Roberta and Darla.

She admired it for a moment, then stuck it in her purse and pulled out a cell phone.

"Do you mind if I take a selfie with you?"

She stepped beside me where I was standing at the bar and I stepped away from it. If she posted it online I didn't want the distinctive bar to give away my location.

"Let's go over here where the light is better."

I steered her to an innocuous wall and she leaned in close to me with a big grin and shot the picture.

"I hope you don't mind, but I'm going to post this to my Facebook page. Otherwise, no one will believe me." She started punching buttons on her phone.

"Go right ahead," I said. "But don't say where we are. I wouldn't want you to get in trouble."

"Oh, you're right. I'll just say we were in Grafton. Thanks!"

"I think I might have left my phone in a bathroom down the hall," I told her. "I'll be right back."

She nodded and waved in my direction, absorbed in her phone. I slipped through the archway and ran quickly down the hallway so I wouldn't be followed. I paused for a moment when I reached the oak door, then turned the knob. Once again, it was unlocked, and I stepped inside and closed the door softly behind me.

The room was dark and quiet and had a somber feel to it. It looked the same as it had the night before. The daylight did not reveal any clues. I sat down on the bed and closed my eyes, concentrating. Nothing. I was beginning to feel ridiculous, but it was in that moment that the closet door at the side of the room caught my attention. The oak finish began, before my very eyes, to turn into a bare, rough plywood, and then the whole room began to transform, with a frightening clarity, into a room that I recognized from my childhood. An unfinished spare room next to the bedroom I shared with Rachael.

I'd had to walk past the door to that room to reach our bedroom every day. And there had come a time, around the advent of the visions and dreams, when that door had begun to beckon to me. There were times when I watched it creep open of its own accord as I approached. Most people would rationalize that away with explanations of loose hinges and air currents and the like. But I knew better. There was an irresistible pull of the unknown emanating from that room, and one day my curiosity succumbed to it.

It was filled with the type of stored items you normally see in an attic and I stood in the middle of that semi-dark room, a young girl on the cusp between innocence and sexual awakening, and watched those closet doors swing open. The lure of that closet was reminiscent of the bluff house itself, in my later dreams, but in that moment of reality, I did not resist. I felt myself walking towards it, and the next thing I remember was lying nearly naked inside it on the cold tile floor with a seductive voice calling to me from the depths of the closet. It whispered my name.

I lay curled on that cold tile, frozen in abject horror. And then I reached inside myself for the strength to pull my sundress back over my head and crawled out of that closet and back into the hallway, closing the door firmly behind me.

And now in the bluff house, I watched this new closet door swinging open and I jumped up from that bed and out into the hallway and made my way quickly back to the great room.

"I was just about to come looking for you, you were taking so long. Did you find the phone?" Roberta asked.

"I did." I pulled my cell phone out of my pocket, flashed it at her and tucked it back away. "I can't thank you enough," I said as I hurried towards the front door.

"No problem. I'm glad you found it. It was really nice to meet you!"

I practically ran out the front door, got to my car as quickly as possible and drove back down the private drive at a dangerous rate of speed, praying I wouldn't run into one of the Ramirez men returning home. When I reached the access road, I stopped holding my breath and relaxed. Jewel was no longer at the church, so I pulled over and texted her that I hadn't found Nicole yet and was heading back to La Vista.

I debated returning to the market to see if Nicole was back yet, but didn't want to alarm June, so I went home and tried her phone again. Still no answer. I practically jumped out of my skin when my phone rang while I was still holding it.

"Nic?"

"No, it's Derek. Are you okay? You sound stressed out."

"Hi. I'm just kind of worried about Nicole. I went to the market and found out she left with Ramirez and forgot her phone. I don't know where she is."

"She's fine. He just dropped her off. I imagine you'll be hearing from her soon."

"Oh. How do you know that?"

"Well, I wasn't sure if I should tell you this, because I didn't want to upset you. I had my private investigator follow them today. Jack is an old military buddy of mine. He works exclusively for a few select clients. He's very reliable, and very discreet. He said they dropped Angelique off at the theater project to meet up with your contractor. Jack stayed with Nicole and Ramirez. Apparently, she just gave him a driving tour of the downtown area. They stopped for a stroll on the marina boardwalk, then he dropped her off at the market. I hope you're not angry with me."

"Well, I'm touched that you were looking out for my friend's safety, but I wish you had told me."

"Fair enough. I'm sorry. I just wasn't sure if you understood the level of danger these people are involved in. I imagine it all sounds a little crazy to you, but things like that happen every day, all over the world. Jack and I saw some pretty bad stuff in the special forces."

"I hear you, and I don't trust any of them."

"Good. You'll be safer that way. I'm going to be out of pocket on business for a couple of days, but you can always reach me on my cell, day or night. Will you call me if anything happens to worry you? If I can't get there right away, I can always send Jack."

"Thank you. I appreciate that. Are you going to London?"

"No, just up to Chicago. It shouldn't take long. I'll call you tomorrow, okay?"

"Okay. Good night, Derek."

"Good night, girl."

No man had called me girl in a long time. I liked it, coming from him. And I was surprised at how disappointed I felt to think I wasn't going to see him for a couple of days. Just as he predicted, I heard from Nicole almost immediately.

"I see that you've tried to call several times," she said. "God, I'm sorry. That is so unlike me to forget my phone. I guess I was distracted. But I'm just fine. I'm home now and they're both gone."

"Well, how did it go?"

"They were actually very professional. They seem genuinely interested in investing in some redevelopment in the area. I told them I have too much on my plate right now to team up with them, and gave them the names of a couple of reputable architects. It just seemed like the natural thing to do in this situation."

"Sure, I can see that," I said, "but I would feel better if Ramirez just moved on. Derek doesn't trust him. He says he's been suspected of being involved in some illegal business, some of it pretty dirty."

"Like what?"

"Suspicion of transporting stolen goods, for one thing. And Derek thinks he might even have connections to the sex trade in foreign countries – maybe even the unsolved disappearance of his fiancée."

She was quiet for a moment, then finally said, "That's an ugly allegation. What makes him say that?"

"Apparently, some business dealings Ramirez had with people in the trade and gut instinct, at this point. Did they talk about David, or the ruby necklace?"

"Yes. Angelique brought up the subject. She thought it was very clever and somewhat amusing that you incorporated David's pet legend into your novel. She spoke very respectfully about your writing career and sounded like she admires you. She didn't say anything about being related to you."

"Well, anyway, I'm glad you're not going to see them again. Do you know why Angelique was meeting with Jamie?"

"How did you know that?" she asked.

I told her about stopping by the Paramount, but not about Derek's investigator. I was certain she would find that intrusive, just as I would. I don't generally keep secrets from Nicole and I knew that I would tell her eventually, but I didn't want to color her opinion of Derek right off the bat. I liked him more than I had liked any man in a long time.

"I'm not certain, but it sounds like Jamie is seriously considering teaming with them for a project," she said. "I'm sorry. I don't imagine you're happy to hear that. Angelique strikes me as a woman who can be very persuasive with men."

"Yeah. Well, Jamie is a big boy and he and I are past history. He'll have to take care of himself. Do you want to have lunch tomorrow?"

"Tomorrow won't work. Maybe we could go shoot at the range the next day?"

"Okay, that sounds good."

"I'm a little tuckered out," she said. "I'll call you on Monday."

At loose ends, I fixed a glass of iced tea and sat down at my computer to check my email. My publicist had several emails that she thought I should answer personally. I spent some time responding to them and then took a call from my agent, Myron.

"How is the new book coming along?"

"I'm still in percolate stage, Myron. You know it takes me a few months to get my thoughts together before a book starts taking shape. It will come together when it's supposed to." I'm not an outliner. That would take the fun out of writing for me.

"It's a good thing you're not working on contract. I'd have to advise you to plant your tush at the computer and percolate till the pot is full."

"Well," I laughed, "I'm in the process of planning a trip to L.A. to do some research. I feel certain that will help solidify the plot for me."

"Speaking of L.A., I'd like to start trying to shop the movie rights for *Desert Queen*. That okay with you?" he asked.

"I insist on retaining final approval of the screenplay and major casting decisions, but I'm open to a movie if the right people come on board."

"Well, I think the best approach is to get a strong lead actress attached to the project," he said. "Maybe one who has her own production company, and then a good director would be more likely to come on board, and the financing would follow. Let's both start thinking about actresses to approach. Now, what have you got going on tomorrow? The Barnes and Noble at Ladue Crossing in St. Louis has asked if you could make an appearance. They had another author lined up, but she got sick and had to back out. Can you fill in, read a few passages, do a Q&A?"

"Sure, no problem."

"I'll set it up and email you the details. Go back to percolating."

I took his advice and spent some time researching online. I knew that I wanted the story to feature a woman in trouble in a mysterious location. I went into my online journal and jotted a list of ideas for the central plot and some possible subplot arcs.

Then I went to the bookcase to pull out my books and decide on what to read at the bookstore the next day. My eye caught on a book about the science of dreaming, written by a psychologist who worked at Harvard Medical School, and was considered an expert in dreams, imagery and hypnosis. I recalled seeing this volume on Jewel's bookshelf. I wondered if she knew anyone who had experienced something similar to what I had in that spare room closet.

I had a sudden, vivid memory of the fear I had felt in that bedroom in the Ramirez house. It seemed that some dark force was reaching out to me, but I was determined not to succumb to it. I would summon the strength I had found as a girl to walk past that spare room on a daily basis. I never entered it again.

*****

Chapter 16

The next morning, I took special care with my hair and makeup, and dressed in a nice pair of black slacks, white silk sleeveless shell and red Jimmy Choo pumps. Those pumps make me feel powerful and I always wear them when I need a little extra boost of confidence. I applied a red lipstick to match and added silver jewelry. Satisfied with the mirror, I grabbed a lightweight pinstripe jacket, in case they had the air conditioning cranked in the store, and headed out.

There was a pretty good crowd at the bookstore, considering they'd had little time to advertise the change in authors. I started out by reading a couple of short essays from my collection, but nothing too heavy, and then read a passage from *The Desert Queen*. Then I opened the floor for questions.

"When did you know you wanted to be a writer?"

"I had always dabbled with it growing up, but didn't seriously consider it until I was studying psychology. My internship in a counseling center gave me the opportunity to hear women's issues up close and personal. I realized I could bring attention to gender struggles as a writer, while exercising my creativity. Who's next?"

"Do you consider yourself a feminist?"

"It depends on your definition. I'm an advocate for the fair treatment of women. I'm appalled that women still generally do not receive equal pay for equal work, and that there are still places in this world where women have few or no rights. But I am not anti-men. I think men are amazing and that God was having a good day when he created men, don't you?"

"I'll say! Have you seen that new Matthew McConaughey movie?" a different woman asked.

"Possibly," I countered, "but my agent advised me not to admit to things like that in public."

That brought a laugh and I pointed to another hand.

"Your last book was more of a thriller. Will you write another?"

"I'm working on a new book which will likely be categorized as a thriller, but in a more contemporary setting. I don't want to say too much on that yet, but it will definitely feature strong women and gender issues. I see a hand in the back."

I couldn't see the woman until the person in front of her shifted to get a look.

"That mysterious ruby was fun in *Desert Queen*," the woman asked. "Where did you get the idea for it?"

It was Angelique. I'd had no idea she was in the crowd and I took a moment to gather myself. She had an innocent smile on her face and people shifted back around and looked at me with interest.

"I don't want to reveal my source, but he was someone very special who had heard it passed around as a local legend."

"Do you mean there are people who actually believe the necklace exists?" Angelique persisted.

I was thinking she missed her calling and should have been a criminal attorney. She had the right air of pretense about her for an effective courtroom style.

"It's surprising the things that people believe. Just look at my second book. That woman believed she would please her husband if she got rid of their infant daughter. Belief is a powerful force, and it's not always driven by logic. Over here."

"Are you saying you think she was a victim?"

"No," I said, "she smothered her baby to death. The child was the victim. But I did want to bring attention to the serious nature of postpartum depression, which is a very real condition that should not be ignored. And that this was an example of one woman taking her desire to please a man to a devastating and mentally unbalanced extreme."

I pointed to another woman who asked how I had landed the interview for the true crime novel. I had successfully changed the subject and I completed the Q&A session without incident. Afterward, I sat at a table up front signing autographs and chatting with people. I didn't see Angelique again until I headed out to the parking lot and found her waiting on a bench on the sidewalk. I walked over, sat down and waited.

"You know," she began, "my mother was very upset to learn that my father might also be your father. She's all about appearances. She grew up in New York society. Her family didn't have a lot of money anymore - her father had lost heavily in the stock market, but she had the right bloodlines and she came out in a debutante party. She first met my father at a society benefit. The proceeds from that party were going to an archaeological society. He came from the right kind of family too. They weren't fabulously wealthy either, but they were highly regarded academics, and my father was a very handsome and charming man with some presence on the world stage." She turned to look at me. "You do resemble him, somewhat. Did he tell you before he died, or did Sophia?"

"It really doesn't matter. I didn't get the chance to know him as I would have liked. That's the part I regret."

"He was a good man," she went on, "but he was too dedicated to his work; always wandering the world looking for bits of junk in the ground. My mother liked the parties and fundraisers but wanted nothing to do with that part of it. She always had male admirers around. I learned about men and what they desire from watching her. Take Derek, for instance. He's obviously attracted to you, but he wants something else too. He still thinks he can find that Mayhall woman. And I imagine he thinks you might be able to provide some clue, considering your connection to the situation, and the novel you wrote. Some people actually do believe that ruby necklace exists. Perhaps he believes he could trade the necklace to get her back. My father might have even been abducted because of the necklace, but who knows in that part of the world? He might have been killed for the cash in his wallet." She turned to look at me again. "Rey is not a man who tolerates intrusion into his business. You would be wise to forget about both him and Derek before you get pulled into something ugly. Why not stick with Jamie Sinclair? He's very attractive and much safer to boot."

"Jamie Sinclair is ancient history for me, Angie."

"Not so ancient. You slept with him once when he was separated from his wife a couple of years ago, didn't you?"

I tried to keep the shock from my eyes when I looked at her. *Had Jamie actually told her that?* It had been a mistake, one for which I had compromised my values and suffered terrible guilt, but at least it had settled my feelings for him once and for all. He was an excellent contractor and a devoted father, but he was susceptible to female attention and still trying to compensate for an overbearing mother by carrying on flirtations with other women, which had led to the separation. I hadn't been able to win his approval as a girl, any more than I'd been able to win the approval of the man who had raised me. Sometimes what we're searching for in someone else is really something we need to find within our own self.

"I don't know what makes you think that and I don't care," I responded. "My personal life is none of your business, and Jamie has a wife and daughter, so be careful about stirring up old news. Why are you really here, Angelique? I'm sure there are plenty of opportunities for Ramirez in other cities; more exciting cities like New York."

"Oh, we'll be heading back to New York when we finish here. My mother is on a flight there now. I just came from dropping her at the airport. She can only tolerate St. Louis for short intervals.

Manhattan is the center of her universe. But Rey is not finished looking around here yet. I just felt compelled to come here today." She gave me a conspiratorial smile. "Maybe it was something I saw in a dream. But sometimes it's best to ignore what you see in a dream." She stood up and looked down at me. "Sometimes what you dream turns into a nightmare."

Then she turned and walked away.

*****

Chapter 17

Sinclair Construction was established on the La Vista riverfront at the turn of the twentieth century during the age of wealthy industrialists who had built the area into a booming hub for shipping materials down the Mississippi, and by rail up to Chicago. Jamie's great grandfather, Joseph Sinclair, had made his reputation on hard, honest work and every Sinclair man who took the helm of the company had to work his way up through the ranks to earn the right. But they also attended the best schools and traveled extensively – the Sinclair version of the well-rounded man.

It's rare to find a contractor in his office on a Sunday, but Jamie was in the habit of spending time there on the weekends when there was no one else around so he could catch up on paperwork, uninterrupted. I spotted his Harley parked behind the chain link fence at the entrance to the construction yard, where the trucks and equipment are stored, and pulled into a parking spot out front. I stepped into the foyer, rang the bell and waited.

After a couple of moments, he appeared in the reception area. I saw him stop in surprise, then he put a smile on his face and made his way forward to open the door for me.

"Hey. Come in. You look nice."

"Thanks. I just came from a book signing. I spotted your bike outside and thought I would stop in to see how you are doing. Do you have a moment?"

"Sure. Let's go in my office."

I thought he looked a little bit wary, but Jamie is well-mannered, if nothing else. Even when he told me he was marrying Elizabeth Hayden, effectively destroying my dreams, he was a perfect gentleman, telling me how much he had enjoyed our time together and wishing me the very best.

We walked past black and white photos, some featuring horse-drawn carriages sporting the Sinclair logo, until we reached his office in the back corner. It was a masculine office with a big desk and leather furniture, and photos of Sinclair projects, Harleys and boats.

"Sit down," he pointed to a leather sofa on the back wall.

I opted for a chair in front of his desk, instead. He took my cue and sat down behind his desk.

"I'm getting excited about the Paramount," I told him. "It looks like we're in the home stretch.

Nicole says everything is on schedule for the projected completion date."

"Actually, we're a bit ahead of schedule now and we're coming in a little under budget too. It's a project we can all be proud of. Nicole told me you've been negotiating with a cinema management company in St. Louis to run it for you. Is that looking like a go?"

"Yes, the lawyers are working on the contract now."

"Are you going to retain ownership or sell it?"

"Well, the management company wants first crack if we decide to sell, but we're going to hang onto it for a little while, just for the novelty. It's probably not practical to keep it in the long run. We'd like to make a profit so we can reinvest in another project."

"Sounds like a plan."

I nodded. "How about you? Any new projects on the horizon?"

He shrugged his shoulders. "Most of our work comes from the hard-bid market, but I think you know that I've been looking at some possible negotiated work with Angelique Vaughn. It sounds like Rey Ramirez has a lot of capital on hand and a solid background in commercial real estate. I saw you at his party," he smiled.

"What do you think of him?"

"I don't really know yet. I have my business development manager checking into his background. But I'm open to the right project. Angelique has represented some clients I'm familiar with in St. Louis. She's very sharp. She says good things about you. Have you known each other long?"

"No, not really," I said. "She's actually what I wanted to talk to you about. Are you sure it's a good idea to work with her? I've heard it suggested that Ramirez has been involved in some shady business deals. Maybe it would be better if they just moved along and left this area to the locals."

He looked surprised for a moment and then he laughed softly. "Angelique warned me you might be jealous that we were spending some time together."

"What? That's not true. She said something to me about that time we were together during your separation. I find that disturbing. Did you tell her that, Jamie?"

"Of course not. Why would I do that? She knows we dated back when we were kids. You must have misunderstood."

"No, I didn't misunderstand."

"Well, you know there was some gossip that went around about us, but that's ancient history."

I nodded. "I'm glad things worked out for you at home. How is Meryl doing? She's starting her first year of college, isn't she?"

"Yeah!" His eyes always lit up when he talked about his daughter. He adored her, and I felt the familiar mix of envy and happiness for a girl who had such a relationship with her father – something I had been denied. "She's going to stay here and attend Lewis and Clark. It was a struggle to get her to agree to college, even though her grades are excellent. She wants to be a model. Liz took her out to Los Angeles to sign with an agency, and they're planning some trips to New York and Paris. She's very interested in high fashion. That's all well and good, but I insisted that she take a regular summer job and learn the value of work and money management. She's been waitressing up at The Loading Dock. That's a fun place and she really enjoys it."

"Modeling. Well, she was always a pretty girl."

"Yeah, I wasn't sure how I felt about that, but she seems very passionate about it. Here's her favorite head shot." He turned and pointed to a photo on the credenza behind his chair.

"Wow. She's really grown up," I said after a moment. "She's beautiful, Jamie."

He smiled. "Your writing career is going gangbusters. I hope your personal life is equally successful."

"We'll see." I stood up. "I hope that you'll be cautious about signing on with outsiders. I think you should do a thorough background investigation. I just have a bad feeling about Ramirez."

"Okay, I've heard you, but I think you're being overly dramatic. Must be the writer in you."

He walked me to the front door and I hurried to my car, fired the engine and headed for the River Road at a reckless rate of speed. I couldn't get away from there fast enough, and it wasn't talking to Jamie that had made me uncomfortable. It was the picture of his daughter. I hadn't seen Meryl Sinclair for several years and girls can change a lot while they're growing up. I couldn't find any words to warn Jamie without sounding even more irrational than he already thought, but I also couldn't shake the sick feeling in the pit of my stomach, because Meryl Sinclair was the young woman in trouble in my dream.

*****

Chapter 18

I stopped off at my house and changed into a casual outfit of capris, a summer top and flat sandals, then I headed for Grafton. The Loading Dock is a wildly popular bar and grill on the waterfront at the entrance to town. It had originally been a boat repair warehouse, but the husband and wife team who had built the Wind Rivers Condos had shrewdly converted it into a gold mine featuring a large open patio by the river and a covered bar, with live bands on weekends. They were both first-rate developments.

As typical for a Sunday, the place was packed out. The parking lot was filled with a mix of Harleys, sports cars and convertibles, and more affordable college kid cars. There was an equal mix of Illinois and Missouri license plates. A blues band was playing from under a tent down by the water.

I threaded my way through the crowd and found a small empty table with an umbrella in the corner of the upper patio by the bar. I kept my Ray Bans on and hoped no one would recognize me. I wanted to keep a low profile.

I scanned the crowd for Meryl Sinclair. The place was jam-packed and I spotted a couple of waitresses, both young and pretty, but not her. Maybe she wasn't working today. After a few moments, a cute little redhead in short shorts stopped by and wiped off my table.

"Sorry for the wait. It's crazy today. What can I get you?"

"Mich Ultra."

"Coming right up."

She melted into the crowd and I turned to watch red and yellow parasails flying over the river behind a speed boat. A middle-aged biker chick passed in front of me and I watched her slip out of the jacket she had worn for the ride to display a tube top, a pierced belly button and too many tattoos. Her figure wasn't bad but she was trying way too hard to look young and edgy, and pretending not to notice that the biker guys were more interested in the college co-eds in the crowd.

"Here you go."

I turned to see my waitress setting down a bottle and a frosted glass. I paid for the beer and included a large tip.

"Thanks!" she smiled.

"You're right," I told her, "it's crazy here. You need more help. Is Meryl working today?"

"Yeah, she's got that section on the other side of the bar. Do you know her?"

"No, but I know her parents. You girls be careful. I'm sure there are lots of strange guys hitting on you in a place like this."

"Ha! Got that right. But lots of cute ones too. Did you want anything to eat?"

"No, I'm good. Thanks."

She walked away and I scanned the other side of the bar for Meryl. After a moment, I spotted her laughing with some young guys at a table out in the sun. She was even more beautiful in person than she was in the head shot. She had inherited her father's blond good looks, magnified, and she had a killer body with a summer tan in the requisite short shorts all the young girls were wearing. I sat sipping my beer, watching her. Everywhere she went, male eyes followed. I was getting that sick feeling back in the pit of my stomach.

My cell phone rang from my purse and I pulled it out and smiled at the readout – Jericho.

"Hey, are you back in St. Louis?" I asked him.

"Driving from Chicago, about halfway back. What are you up to?"

"Sitting at The Loading Dock in Grafton, drinking a beer."

"By yourself?"

"Yes."

"Oh, that's not good," he laughed. "Be wary of oversexed Harley riders."

"I'll keep that in mind. Was your trip a success?"

"In my mind, it was. I turned down a project an acquaintance keeps trying to bring me in on. I took a look, to be polite, but I'm just not interested in that market. I'm sorry I'm not there to keep you company. A beautiful woman should not drink alone."

"I was at loose ends. I did an unscheduled book signing in your neck of the woods, at the Ladue Crossing Barnes and Noble."

"I'm sorry I missed that. Did you have a good crowd?"

"Very good, but some of them were expecting another writer," I laughed.

"Well, I'm sure you didn't disappoint. You're a terrific writer."

"Really? Have you read any of my books?"

"All three of them. All three fascinating in different ways."

"*You* read *The Desert Queen*?"

"Sure. Why does that surprise you?"

"Well, that's not a typical guy kind of novel."

"I beg to differ. You did an excellent job with the action sequences. And I liked how you handled the sex. It wasn't like a romance novel. It was more like how a man would write sex."

Just listening to him talk about sex was making my heart beat a little faster, but hearing him talk about the sex scenes that I wrote felt intimate and a little bit naughty.

"Well, I'm going to take that as a compliment."

"It is."

We were both silent for a moment, then he asked what I was doing the next day.

"I think Nicole and I are going to shoot at the range at some point."

"No kidding? You both like to shoot? Why does that not surprise me?"

"Hey, we're not your typical women."

"I heard that. Listen, Jack has a nice outdoor range at his place out in Eureka. Why don't you girls come out there and shoot with us? We can throw some burgers on the grill and make an afternoon of it."

I thought quickly. *Would Nicole be up for that?*

"Well, I'll have to check with Nic. Is Jack going to tell her he was stalking her yesterday?"

He laughed. "He wasn't stalking her, he was protecting her. But let's wait to disclose that until he's had a chance to make friends. Let me check with Jack to set a time, then I'll text you the address. Okay?"

"Okay, sounds good."

His voice took on a husky quality. "I'm looking forward to seeing you again."

"Me too."

We hung up and I took a long chug of my beer, trying to tell myself not to get too excited. This was a man who was still carrying a torch for another woman.

"Hi. Can I get you another Ultra?" It was Meryl Sinclair.

"Oh, no thanks. I'm good."

She smiled and looked me over. "Shannon said you're a friend of my parents. Do I know you?"

"Well, I'm an old friend of your father's and he and I are working on a project together. The Paramount Theatre. Ruby January."

I held out my hand and she shook it.

"Oh, hi! You're the famous writer. My dad said he dated you before he married my mom."

"Yes, he did. That was a long time ago. He was telling me you've been doing some modeling."

"Yeah, I'm really excited about that! My mom and I are planning trips to New York and Paris for the fashion weeks."

"Well, good luck with that. In the meantime, you be careful working here. Lots of men looking to pick up pretty girls in this place. You be especially careful walking out to your car at night."

She laughed. "You sound just like my dad. Don't worry. I'm super careful. Well, I need to get back to work. It was really nice to meet you."

I watched her walk away, and so did every man she passed, although the ones with dates tried to be discreet about it. I was thinking I would be heading out as I watched her pass the bar, then my eyes settled on a man sitting on one of the stools, facing towards me, a smile on his face, and a chill of dread came over me. It was Rey Ramirez. He picked up two beer bottles from the bar and strolled towards me. Even in chinos and a golf shirt he stood out in this crowd like a movie star in a prison yard. He set an Ultra on my table and held onto the Corona in his other hand.

"What a lovely surprise. May I join you, Ruby?"

"Of course."

He sat down and seemed to be gathering his thoughts for a moment.

"I was disappointed that your friend Nicole cannot partner with me for a project."

"Well, she's very popular, and very busy right now."

"Yes, but not too busy to partner with Jericho, it seems."

I shrugged. "I guess he beat you to the punch."

"That seems to be happening frequently."

"Well, that might have something to do with Angelique. I'm under the impression she enjoys pitting the two of you against one another."

"And why do you think that is?" he asked.

"A game of power, perhaps? One where she's holding the high card?"

He smiled and set the Corona down on the table, his long fingers toying with the bottle for a moment. "That's a dangerous game to play. Sometimes a player is holding a secret card under the table." His eyes came back up to mine. "Qué te gusta secretos, Ruby?"

"Eso depende de quién está manteniendo el secreto."

"Yes," he laughed. "It certainly depends on who is keeping the secret. Your Spanish is better than you originally indicated."

"I learned most of my Spanish from a lecherous architect who spent his summers in Mexico," I told him. "Not the best choice. He wanted to teach me helpful phrases like, 'Can I dance naked on your drafting table?' and 'We'd like a bottle of tequila and a room upstairs.'"

He threw back his head and laughed and I was reminded of how much charisma he had and how dangerous that could be for an innocent young girl.

"A man after my own heart." He leaned forward and gave me the full force of those dark eyes. "Do you think I am holding a secret, Ruby? You made a clandestine trip to my house yesterday."

I leaned forward and held his gaze. "Did you make a clandestine trip to *my* house? Do you think *I* am holding something secret?"

He leaned back in his chair and smiled. "Angelique has underestimated you. I believe she feels threatened by the male interest you attract, but she does not view you as cunning enough to be her equal. She is obviously mistaken."

He picked up his Corona and tipped the bottle to his lips, drained it and set it back down.

"How did you know about my visit to your house?" I asked him. "Are *you* holding a secret card under the table?"

"Perhaps I'm holding it in a deep, dark closet where the light is silent." His smile was knowing and seductive.

"But the darkness is not? Did you answer when the darkness whispered your name, Rey?"

The smile on his face turned cold.

"There, you see. You do know the right questions to ask. The game just took an interesting turn, don't you agree? Buen dia, Ruby."

He stood and made his way through the crowd towards the parking lot. On the way, he passed Meryl Sinclair unloading a tray of sandwiches at a table full of admiring college-aged boys. He didn't appear to notice her. I watched her fending off passes good-naturedly as colorful parasails floated in a blue sky behind her, and the band played a soulful version of "Hoochie Coochie Man."

*****

Chapter 19

The next day I rode shotgun in Nicole's Navigator. It hadn't been difficult to convince her to go. The thought of shooting with two former Navy Seals was right up her alley. When they suggested we could bring our dogs to run the property, that was the cherry on top. Ginger and Jonah hung deliriously out the two back windows, taking in the sights and smells.

Eureka is a suburb of St. Louis out Interstate 44. It's best known for the Six Flags St. Louis amusement park, but the scenic rocky terrain as you start heading southwest in Missouri towards the Ozarks is also a draw.

Jack Boetta's place was in a secluded area with lots of acreage – the kind of place that works well for an outdoor range. The house was an A-frame with a masculine vibe, like its owner. Jack was a nice-looking guy with dark hair and blue eyes and it amused me that he and Nicole were both wearing camouflage tee shirts. Like minds, I supposed. Derek was a little more subtle, wearing an Army green tee with his jeans. I drank in the sight of him, surprised at how much I'd missed him.

Jack explained that the range was a good distance out and we would be riding four-wheelers to get to it. Nicole and I had brought our handguns in concealed carry lockboxes, and the guys stored them in the built-in cases on the four-wheelers and started them up. I climbed on behind Derek, slipped my arms around his waist and heard his surprised, "Well, that's a first. He must really like her," he said over his shoulder.

I followed his gaze to find Jack letting Nicole take the driver's seat and climbing on behind her.

"I should have warned you," I told him. "She has control issues. She always wants to drive, especially on terrain. She started riding dirt bikes as a kid, but she's terrified of flying, where you have no control."

We took off across the field and the dogs ran happily after us.

"Did you ride dirt bikes too?" he called back.

"On the back of hers. I tried learning to drive, but kept popping the clutch and getting dragged down the road. I prefer riding on the back of a motorcycle. I took right to a stick shift in a car, though, and I enjoy driving a four-wheeler."

He turned and grinned at me. "Were you wanting to drive this one, too?"

"No," I shook my head. "I'm happy to ride behind you."

We maneuvered around the bank of a nice little lake and then headed over some trickier terrain through some trees. The range was set into the trees in a secluded area with the targets in front of a steep bank of land that served to catch stray rounds. The guys produced ear muffs from their packs and the dogs wandered farther down the trail towards an open meadow.

"They'll be fine out there," Jack said. "Plenty of rabbits and squirrels to chase."

Jack was shooting a Sig Sauer, and Derek was using a Glock. They approved of our compact guns, and we took turns firing at targets. They were both expert shooters and Nicole did fairly well too. I held my own, hitting more targets than I missed.

Afterward, we rode the four-wheelers over to the meadow to round up the dogs, who had kept their distance from the loud noise. I noted with amusement that Jack was now driving. He must have made a real impression on Nicole with his shooting. The dogs stopped off to splash in the lake and we sat on the patio while Jack built a charcoal fire in the grill. When Nicole went inside with him to help with a salad, Derek suggested we take a stroll down to the lake. I walked along beside him, thinking I couldn't remember a more pleasant day.

"Jack seems like a really nice guy," I told him as he fished some tennis balls from a nearby gazebo.

"Yeah, he's a good guy. Here we go. He used to have a German shepherd, but he died last year. I knew there were some balls around here somewhere."

He started throwing them out over the water for the dogs and they dove after them enthusiastically. Jonah emerged with a ball in his mouth, shaking off the water and dropping it proudly at Derek's feet. He threw the ball and both dogs took off after it.

"Jonah really likes you," I told him. "He's often timid with strange men."

"Why is that? He looks like a tough guy."

"He was hurt by a man he trusted."

He turned to study me silently for a moment. "Why have you never married again?"

"Well, I'm not opposed to the idea, if that's what you're asking. But, in all honesty, I haven't spent a lot of time looking around. I've concentrated on my education, my career, and raising my son. Maybe someday," I smiled at him.

"Jack told me your son is a talented soccer player with a solid right hook," he smiled back at me.

I laughed. "Yes, well he doesn't normally employ it on the soccer field."

"Sounded like it was self-defense. That happens between guys sometimes in contact sports."

I nodded. "What about you? You never wanted to get married until you met Melanie?"

"No. I was all about the military for the longest time, and my picture of marriage had been colored. My father had a wandering eye and my mother eventually divorced him. I saw how much that marriage hurt her. I think I enlisted just to spite him. He wanted me to join his firm after college. I loved being a Seal, but when I finally discharged I didn't know what else to do, so I joined him. It turns out I had a real knack for it. I forgave my father and learned a lot from him before he died."

He stood and we started walking back towards the patio.

"What about Jack? Has he never married either?" I asked.

"Jack was married when he enlisted, but he was even more devoted than I was. She left him when he signed up for a fourth tour. They have a daughter and he has visitation rights. He hasn't seriously dated anyone since but, in all fairness, he works some odd hours. It would take a unique woman to deal with his lifestyle."

I thought about asking him some more about Melanie and what kind of woman she was, but I didn't want to spoil the mood. We rejoined Jack and Nicole and ate a good spread of burgers, Caesar salad and grilled corn. They had a pitcher of lemonade squeezed fresh from Meyer lemons and spiked with good vodka, and we sat on the patio enjoying the breeze and the good company.

Derek asked about our ideas for the hotel and Nicole and I took turns sharing our conception. Derek liked that we intended to return the Stratton to its glory days, with a contemporary twist. It appeared that we would make a good project team.

Nicole took a moment to tease Derek about beating out Angelique and Ramirez for the purchase and he took that opportunity to confess to having Jack follow her and Ramirez to make sure she was okay. I think we all held our breath for a moment, waiting for her reaction, but she took it right in stride, seemingly fascinated that she hadn't a clue she was being tailed. That sparked some good-natured banter between her and Jack and when I sneaked a glance at Derek, he winked at me.

When we decided it was time to head out, I heard Jack telling Nicole she was welcome to come out and shoot anytime and I smiled to myself as Derek walked me around front, where we loaded the dogs into the back seat.

"Anything new to report on Ramirez?" he asked.

I shook my head. I wasn't ready to tell him about my dream or what I had seen at Aeries the day that Sophia died. People tend to laugh off things like that.

"I saw him at The Loading Dock yesterday and we spoke briefly. He mentioned being disappointed about the hotel, but that's about it," I said, not wanting to alarm him.

"Well, you stay away from him anyway, okay?"

"Is that an order?" I teased.

He took my hand in his and squeezed it. "No. But he's a dangerous guy and I don't want anything to happen to you."

I searched those serious green eyes for a moment, then reached up to plant a kiss. This time I didn't aim for his cheek. I had been looking at his mouth off and on all afternoon and couldn't resist the urge. He returned the pressure, and then I turned and climbed into the passenger seat. Nicole started the engine and I risked a glance at him. He smiled at me as we backed out of the drive and headed out.

I looked over at Nicole. She had a soft, private smile on her face. I hadn't seen her look like that since Kyle was alive and I tried to be careful not to intrude.

"I had a good time. I hope you did too."

"Yes. Jack is a decent guy. I like him."

"I hope you're not upset about him following you. I'm sure Derek had the best of intentions. He honestly believes Ramirez was involved in the disappearance of his fiancée."

Nicole could relate to the trauma of losing someone you loved. She was silent for a moment as she navigated the secondary road back towards the interstate.

"I'm not upset. There actually was something strange that happened with Ramirez. I didn't want to say anything about it because it will probably sound ridiculous, but after we dropped Angelique, we took a walk down by the marina. We sat down to chat on a bench and I remember looking at him while he was asking me a question. I think it was something about you, but I can't remember what. The next thing I knew he was helping me off the bench to return to the car, but I can't remember what we talked about while we were sitting there."

"Well," I said, "it sounds like a short conversation. You must have been distracted."

"That's just it." She shot me a look. "The last thing I remember before we sat down was checking the time on the tower clock over the marina. When he helped me off the bench, it was 15 minutes later."

I looked at her, at a loss, for a moment.

"What are you saying? Do you think he drugged you? Do you think he slipped something in your drink at lunch?"

"No, no," she shook her head. "There was no opportunity for that, and I didn't feel like I was drugged. I just can't remember any of the conversation from the bench. That's weird, don't you think?" I wasn't sure what to say and after a moment, she laughed it off. "I'm too young for Alzheimer's, but I am having some PMS issues this week. Maybe it was just a bad case of brain fog."

We both fell silent, lost in our own thoughts. I was remembering what Ramirez had said about the game taking an interesting turn. I decided it was time that I try to put a name to the game and figure out the rules, before the next turn came around.

*****

Chapter 20

Nicole dropped us at home and Jonah headed right for his favorite armchair to take a nap. I put my gun away and sent a text to Jewel, asking if she was up for some company. She was and I headed up the River Road, thinking I hadn't made this many trips to Grafton in years. It's funny how people or places come back into prominence in your life. This little town had been the center of my universe when I was younger, then I had avoided it for a number of years, and now it was drawing me back with an unsettling regularity.

Jewel was waiting on her porch with a pitcher of iced tea and we sat sipping and listening to the creek for a moment.

"What are your plans? I asked. "Are you going to keep this house and stay on here for awhile?"

"I don't have any plans to sell this house. I don't need the money and I enjoy coming back here for visits. I have friends in this area, including you now," she smiled at me. "But I'll eventually be drawn back to Europe. I feel most at home there."

I felt sad at the prospect of losing her company, but understood the draw to the place that feels like home. I love to travel and explore, but I'm always relieved to see those limestone bluffs when I return. It's comforting.

"What can you tell me about Angelique's childhood?" I finally asked.

"Well, she didn't lack for anything materially. She attended good private schools in New York, then came to St. Louis to attend Wash U, I believe in an attempt to connect more with David. He was gone a lot with his work and their relationship was strained. He felt that Cassandra manipulated the girl and worked to keep a distance between them when he was home. He always thought there was something sad and strange about Angelique, but he couldn't get close enough to her to find out why, and eventually Cassandra's coldness and flirtations with other men would drive him back to his work. He was utterly devoted to archaeology. I would go for long periods without hearing anything from him, as well."

"Did she have any experiences with dreams or visions, or anything unusual like that?" I asked.

"David told me he had seen evidence of that, but I never got a chance to talk to her about it. Cassandra had poisoned her towards me and she's always kept her distance. But I am not surprised that she's gifted, since you and she are half-sisters. It has been my experience that gifts like that tend to run in families."

"Sophia told me that Richard Vaughn was not David's natural father; that she'd had a love affair with another man, whom I believe was named Marek. Did you know that?"

She was silent for a moment. "Sophia did not share that with me directly. But David told me she had revealed that to him shortly before he disappeared. I believe it caused something of a rift between them towards the end."

"She seemed to think there was something extraordinary about Marek," I told her.

"Such as?"

"I don't know. She was trying to tell me about him when she had the heart attack. I think I saw him in a vision."

She was silent for another moment. "Who do you believe he was?" she finally asked.

"I have no idea," I said.

She watched me thoughtfully for a moment.

"Do you believe in the supernatural realm, Ruby - the realm of light?"

"Yes, I do," I nodded, "but also the realm of darkness. I have occasionally experienced that too. When you have a gift such as mine, the darkness whispers to you, as well as the light."

She leaned forward and held my eyes for a long moment. "What if I suggested to you that Marek came from the realm of light? That he was not of this world, and that was why it was forbidden for

Sophia to be with him, and why he had to leave when they broke that sacred law?"

I looked at her, confused, for a moment. "Do you mean like the Nephilim that are mentioned in the Old Testament? When the sons of God coupled with the daughters of men, because they could not resist their beauty?"

"Yes," she nodded. "Their offspring were said to be renowned. In what ways is not explained, other than some of them being strong."

"They were reportedly wiped out in the ancient flood. Are you suggesting that such a thing has occurred again?"

"That is what Sophia believed. It's what she told David."

"What did David make of that?"

"David was an archaeologist. His life revolved around legends and hidden truths. I have spoken with a few other gifted individuals who also held that belief." She shrugged her shoulders. "It is within the realm of possibility, Ruby. If you believe the scriptures, there are dark powers and principalities who rule on Earth, and also angels of light who are assigned here as watchers, who sometimes intervene in the affairs of men and women. They were said to be able to disguise themselves as mortals. Perhaps they still walk among us. That would explain the unusual abilities of certain people," she smiled at me.

I said nothing for a moment, then shook my head. "Well, it isn't likely we will discover the truth about anything like that until we die."

"You may be right," she said with a smile, and then returned to sipping her tea and gazing out over the creek.

I fell silent as I recalled the last conversation I'd had with Sophia, when we had both seen the image of her mysterious paramour. There had been something so unique about him. I had sensed it in that brief glimpse before my grandmother had collapsed.

I was still pleasantly relaxed from the spiked lemonade, and the soothing trickle of water moving over rocks in the creek was making me sleepy. I closed my eyes and drifted into a dreamlike state.

I could still hear the water and I followed the sound to a footbridge and crossed the creek into a meadow. There was a man standing with his back to me and, as he turned to me, the light broke through the trees and I saw his face. It was Marek. He didn't speak but there was a quality emanating from him that was unlike anything I had ever experienced, except perhaps in a dream — something so powerful and secure. I didn't want to leave him but a loud noise awakened me suddenly and I looked around in a daze and saw Jewel picking up the bamboo tray from the porch, where it appeared to have fallen from the table.

"Did you enjoy your nap?" she smiled at me.

"How long was I asleep?" I asked her.

"Not long," she said. "Were you dreaming of Marek?" she asked. "You spoke his name out loud."

"Did I?"

She nodded and I searched my mind for the dream, trying to hold onto the fading fragments.

"I saw him, Jewel. Just as clearly as I did in the vision at the winery. What does all of this mean?"

"You are the only one who can answer that, Ruby. Whatever you believe you discovered there is for you and no one else," she said.

She returned to rocking her chair and watching the creek, and I did the same. We sat silently on the porch sipping tea and listening to the water move over the rocks until the afternoon shadows deepened into evening.

*****

Chapter 21

The dream was lucid. I was on the second story balcony of my childhood home, watching my mother entertain guests in the living room below. The men were all flirting with her and paying her compliments. She outshone the few women in the room, whom I believed had been carefully selected for their more average looks and personalities.

Dismayed, I returned to my bedroom. It was late at night, but I wasn't sleepy, so I switched on the bedside lamp and opened the novel I was reading – *The Thorn Birds*. I was drawn to the story of an older woman desiring a younger, attractive man who was forbidden because he was a priest, and the young, innocent woman who was inadvertently caught in an illicit triangle. I had an odd sensation of having read it before, though I was certain I had not.

I was engrossed in the story and didn't notice the door opening until he was inside my room, closing it behind him. I recognized the man – Jay Delacroix, a wealthy businessman of whom my mother was overly fond. I didn't like him, or the way he looked at me whenever I ran into him with my mother – the same way he was standing beside my bed, looking at me now.

"What are you doing?" I asked. "Get out of here or I'll call for my mother."

He smiled and before I could react, he dropped onto my bed and put his hand over my mouth, holding me down. He smelled of liquor and too much aftershave.

"Don't play games with me, princess. You might fool those other schmucks with your haughty looks, but I know what you want. You want the same thing every beautiful girl wants from a powerful man. I've just been waiting for the right opportunity to give it to you."

I bit his hand on my mouth and he howled in pain and pulled it away. A second later, he hit me across the face with a stunning force for someone who was drunk and I fell back into the pillows in a daze of pain and fear.

"You make a sound and I'll tell your mother you lured me into your bed to spite her," he seethed at me. "She'll believe me too. Just try it and see."

He pulled up my nightgown and started tugging at my panties, and I pushed against him in earnest, but the weight of his big, stocky body was too much, and I choked on fear when he managed to pull them off.

Then his hot mouth was on mine and I felt a stabbing, searing pain between my legs. He started thrusting wildly and mumbling incoherent words in my ear. I was frozen in a state of shock and pain. Somewhere in the distance I heard the muted sound of my mother's laughter.

When he was finished, he climbed clumsily out of my bed, repeating his warning that if I told anyone, he would say that I seduced him when he was drunk. Then he smiled and winked as he told me we could make this a regular thing and he would make it worth my while – that he could give me things that boys my age could not.

After he was gone, I stumbled into the bathroom, trying to ignore the pain between my legs, and vomited into the toilet. Then I took a hot shower. I knew you weren't supposed to wash away the evidence, but it didn't matter, because there was no way I was going to subject myself to the humiliation and futility of a rape trial with a rich man and his clever lawyers. I put on fresh nightclothes, changed the sheets on the bed, and lay in the darkness, sick in my soul.

My mother peeked in the door on her way to bed and asked why I was awake so late. I looked at her standing there with a smile on her face and desperately wanted her to comfort me. I started to say, in a halting voice, that there was something I wanted to tell her about Jay Delacroix. Then I watched her smile turn into a frozen mask and she interrupted to say he had told her I had been flirting with him and that she didn't want to hear anymore on the subject – that I should stick to boys my own age, lest I garner an ugly reputation. Then she closed the door and I was alone in the dark.

As I lay there, the pain inside me coiled into something hard and impenetrable. I decided no man was ever going to take advantage of me again. My last thought before I fell into an exhausted, dreamless state of sleep was of my mother's face when I had reached out to her for help. Except that it wasn't the face of my mother. It was Cassandra Vaughn's face. I was sixteen. I was Angelique.

*****

Chapter 22

It was just after dawn, my favorite time of day. Jonah and I were on the lower portion of the La Vista Park trail. A hot August temperature was forecast, so we had come out early for a walk and I stood on the wooden bridge, watching him splash through the creek again. After a few moments, I became aware of a jogger approaching from the River Road side of the trail. I somehow knew I would see Angelique there. She pulled up and took a moment to catch her breath before leaning against the rails next to me. We both watched my dog for a time, saying nothing.

"He seems to have recovered from the attack," she finally said.

I looked at her for a moment, thinking how much she and Rachael had in common, these two attractive half-sisters of mine who had both been violated by men when they were innocent young girls. I hadn't been able to help Rachael, but it wasn't too late for Angelique.

"It's possible to survive an attack and not be bitter, Angie." I looked into her eyes for a moment. "Not all men are abusive. There are men in the world who are good and kind and strong, and they can enrich your life, if you'll let them."

"Like Derek?" I caught the subtle sarcasm in her tone.

"Just because Derek was not the right man for you doesn't mean you won't find one who makes you happier than he ever could. I used to think Jamie Sinclair was the man for me and I wasted a lot of time and emotion pining away for him – a man who was out of my reach and who was not right for me after all. Sometimes it's the challenge of winning someone that is drawing us more than the person. Sometimes we're just trying to recover what we believe someone else took away from us. You're a unique person, Angelique. Don't waste your gifts on petty matters."

She looked at me for a moment. "You and I are not the only ones. Ramirez is powerful and it takes all of my wits to keep him in check. And there are others. Not many, but a few." She looked back at Jonah. "Rey has very strong powers of persuasion – with women, to be sure, but even stronger with animals. Animals have an innate understanding of the chain of command. Rey knew about your dog's fear and he wanted to test you, to see what you could do. I've seen what he's capable of, so I persuaded him to let me do it."

I looked at her, horrified. "Are you saying you sent that Rottweiler after Jonah?"

"If I hadn't, Rey would have, and the results would have been ugly, trust me. If you hadn't diverted that dog, I would have called him off. I wasn't going to let your dog get hurt."

Something primitive rose up inside of me from my time spent in the back alleys of Grafton as a kid, and I struggled against the urge to hit her with a right cross. She must have sensed my intention because she backed away and held up her hand.

"I was trying to help you that day, whether you believe it or not," she said, and I caught her furtive glance up the path. "Jamie Sinclair turned down our offer to form a joint venture yesterday. Rey believes you influenced that decision and he'll be looking to pay you back for that. He's already suspicious of me. If I help you, he'll come after me, and I'm trying to find out if he was responsible for our father's death. Just be on your guard." Then she turned and jogged back towards the River Road.

I spun around and looked up the path. There was nothing there, but it was eerily quiet and I now had a sense of impending danger. The hill was the only way back to my car. If there was something or someone coming, maybe we could beat them back to it, or maybe there would be other people on the trail by now. I patted the knife sheath on my thigh to reassure myself, glad that I had strapped it on, and called for Jonah.

We moved quickly up the trail, but just as we reached the bottom of the hill, I saw the wolf. Wolf sightings were rare in this area, but their population had been making a slow comeback, since being hunted to near extinction decades ago. He was running down an ancillary path that ends near the bottom of the hill and is marked with Private Property signs, as it leads to a Catholic priests' retreat in the bluffs.

I sensed Jonah's fear and uncertainty but forced myself to relax while I unsnapped my sheath. Jonah had moved off the trail, into the brush, and was watching me nervously. In that moment, I decided it was time for Jonah to face his fear and regain his identity. I felt certain he would come to my aid if he saw me in trouble.

I pulled out my dagger and braced myself as the wolf launched itself in the air. He came down on top of me and I made a quick thrust for his side. It just grazed him and his teeth clamped down on my wrist. I cried out in pain as the dagger fell from my hand. I managed to get my foot under him and push him off me. I didn't see my knife, but there was a thick, sturdy stick in the grass next to me. I picked it up and whacked him across the snout with all the force I could muster and he pulled back, stunned. I went for another blow with the stick, but this time he was ready and clamped down onto it, pulling it from my grasp.

Before he could launch at me, Jonah suddenly came flying into him. They fell into a snarling, biting tangle and I looked around frantically for my dagger. I finally spotted it in the leaves and grabbed it up and went after the wolf, who now had Jonah pinned with his teeth clamped onto his neck.

This time I landed a short thrust into his side, just deep enough to send a message. He released Jonah and howled in pain, shocked out of his trance.

"Get," I commanded, and this time he obeyed and disappeared over the embankment.

Jonah struggled up to a sitting position and I sat down next to him and checked his neck. This time the skin was broken, although not badly, and I was glad I had kept his shots up to date.

Jonah had emerged from the belly of the whale, so to speak, and had faced his fear. I pulled him against me, wrapping my arm around him gingerly. He gave me a kiss and we sat there collecting ourselves for a moment. I wiped my blade off in the grass and put it back in the sheath, then we headed back for the car. I decided we'd had enough of this trail for awhile. I understood Angelique's caution towards Ramirez. Under that charm was a dangerous personality.

Derek thought Ramirez had sold his fiancée into the sex trade, and I now believed he was capable of something that heinous. I was worried that Meryl

Sinclair might be in danger of the same fate, and I suspected I was going to get the opportunity to face my fear, as well.

*****

Chapter 23

I asked Jewel to meet me for lunch at the A&W Restaurant in Grafton. I parked in the corner of the lot and waited for her in my car. When she pulled in next to me, I got out and pointed to the tables under a shade tree.

"I know it's really hot today, but do you mind if we sit outside?"

"Not at all," she said. "I don't mind the heat as much as most people."

We settled in at a table and a waitress came almost immediately for our order. We decided on tomato burgers and frosty mugs of root beer.

"That's what I always ordered here as a kid," I told her. "This place was known as the 'root beer stand' to the locals and still had curb service, if you remember."

"Yes, it was designed as one of the original drive-ins – one of the last of its kind, as I recall."

I nodded. "Rachael was a curb hop here for the couple of summers she was old enough to work before we had to move. I used to come here and eat at the counter so I could watch Rachael work. The customers all liked her so much."

I sat silently reminiscing for a moment, then got to the point.

"I noticed you have some works about the science of dreams on your bookshelves," I said. "So do I. I was wondering if you believe the concepts of lucid dreaming, control of dreams and dreams within dreams are realistic?"

The waitress arrived with our order and Jewel watched me thoughtfully while she set it out and left.

"Has something happened, Ruby? What are you concerned about?

"Angelique does have some of the same abilities that I do. I'm not sure to what extent."

"Are you concerned that Angelique is your adversary and may try to use her abilities against you?"

"No," I shook my head. "Surprisingly, I believe she's been trying to help me, although her methods are questionable. It's Rey Ramirez I'm concerned about."

I reminded her of what happened on the deck at Aeries. I told her I wasn't sure that the vision had originated with me and about the strange sensation I'd felt when Ramirez pointed his fingers towards me. Then I described the animal attacks on the trail. I watched the concern on her face deepen as I talked.

"What happened at the winery sounds like telepathic projection, also known as thoughtform projection," she said. "It's a very rare ability to form a picture of something – usually a person, whether living or deceased, and project it into the open where it can be seen by someone else. It's extremely rare, but I've encountered one person who could do things like that. She had a disturbed personality. When I tried to dissuade her from using that ability for personal gain, she terminated our relationship. The sensation you felt sounds like energy projection. That's even less common." She watched me carefully for a moment. "I would advise you to keep your distance from Ramirez, Ruby. He sounds dangerous and unbalanced."

"It's not that simple." I told her about the dream and my belief that Meryl Sinclair might be in danger. "It also seems evident that he is pursuing me for a number of reasons, so I don't think I'm going to be able to avoid him."

"Well, the best defense is a good offense, as they say. I suggest you start trying to explore any latent abilities you might not be aware of yet." She reached over and squeezed my hand. "I also think you should stick close to Derek Jericho. He's a good person to have around in a dangerous situation."

I was sure that was true and that was one more excuse to see him again. There was an undeniable attraction between us that was starting to deepen into something meaningful, and I wanted to tread carefully.

"How's your burger?" I asked her.

"It's really good," she smiled, letting me change the topic. "That's obviously a homegrown tomato — so much better than the grocery store variety."

We finished our lunch in companionable conversation, but my thoughts were distracted with questions about Ramirez. It was comforting to know I had support from good friends, but I had a feeling it was going to boil down to a contest of wits and skill between Ramirez and me. I hoped I would be up to the challenge.

*****

Chapter 24

I pulled into St. Patrick's on my way home and walked over to the red front doors. They were open. I went in and made my way to a stand of candles to the side of the altar and lit three – each one for a different woman.

Jewel was right. There was something special about having a sacred space to yourself. I knelt in a pew and prayed quietly for each of the women, who had all three been violated by men. The first was Melanie Mayhall, who may or may not have been alive. Her fate was unknown to me, but if she was still alive and in peril, I prayed she would be found. The second was Angelique. I prayed she would find the strength to overcome the pain of being raped, and then betrayed by her own mother. The third candle was for Rachael. I don't know if it makes any difference to light a candle and pray for someone who has already passed over, but I lit it anyway and prayed she was happy.

I left the church feeling more peaceful. As I walked through the red doors, my phone vibrated. It was Derek and I sat down on the steps and answered.

"I've got this charity thing I need to go to on Friday night and I was hoping you would go with me," he told me. "It's a Roaring 20s casino night at the Thaxton – a speakeasy in downtown St. Louis. I have to mingle with the money crowd occasionally for my business, but this is a benefit for an animal shelter. I thought you would appreciate that."

"That sounds like fun, and I do love animal charities. Jonah was a shelter dog. Are we supposed to dress Roaring 20s, then?"

"Absolutely. Are you up for that?"

"Absolutely."

"Great," he laughed softly.

We sat silently for a moment.

"What are you doing?" he asked. "Writing?"

"No, I just stopped into St. Patrick's in Grafton. It's the church I grew up in. I was thinking about my sister Rachael and I wanted to light a candle for her." I hesitated for a split second. "I lit one for Melanie too."

There was silence for a moment.

"That was nice of you." He sounded genuinely touched.

I sat on the steps of my childhood church and shared with him the pain of not knowing how Rachael had come to fall from the bluffs, and that she had been troubled and I didn't know how to help her. He listened sympathetically and shared his pain of not knowing what had happened to

Melanie and not being able to help her. Our bond was growing deeper. The house where Ramirez was staying was just overhead, but I did not allow that to intrude on our intimacy.

I drove home in a relaxed state of mind. When I got there, I researched Meryl Sinclair on social media. Her Facebook profile was public, and she had actually posted her class schedule, for the benefit of her friends. She was going to have to learn to be more careful about things like that, especially if she went into modeling. She was only taking a few classes this semester and she had listed the general time she was taking them, like English Lit on Thursday morning. But with that information, you could find the time and location of a class on the college website.

The only night class she was taking was Intro to Sociology, which happened to be this very night. It was scheduled for 6:50 to 9:00, but this was the first night of class, so I knew it was probable the professor would merely go over the syllabus, give the first assignment and dismiss early.

I timed it so I would arrive a half-hour into class. I didn't know what car Meryl was driving, but since the class was in Baldwin Hall, I speculated she would park in the northern lot, which just happens to be next to campus security. I parked in the corner of the lot, rolled down my window and settled in, sipping the iced tea I had brought along.

It was times like this when I missed the cigarette habit I had kicked years earlier. I quit cold turkey right before I got pregnant with Max but had returned to it briefly when I was going through the divorce.

Twenty minutes later, my patience paid off. Meryl did indeed arrive in this parking lot. She was flanked by two other students. Walking in a crowd was good. She got into a light green, older model Volkswagen Passat that was parked under a street lamp close to the security building – also good. She at least appeared to have a sense of caution about walking around in secluded areas, and I relaxed a little bit as I followed her out of the lot and down the street. I kept my distance as she took a route that I knew led to her neighborhood. When I entered there, I hung back even more. These were pricey homes, set well apart, and it would be easy to get spotted.

She pulled into a drive and up into the garage of a house I knew belonged to Jamie Sinclair. I watched the garage door come down. She was safely inside. There was really nothing more I could do. I certainly couldn't keep following her around indefinitely.

I concentrated on my plans for the next day. I had gotten involved with an organization called Girl Power that sponsored young girls with creative gifts. I was hosting a pool party for them at my house. There was one girl in particular who reminded me of myself when I was her age. We can't go back and change our own past, but we can try to improve the future for someone else, and perhaps find some measure of redemption in that.

*****

Chapter 25

My pool was full of girl power – mostly high school girls, but also a few in middle school, ages 12 through 14 – those awful years of change. Some were unabashedly worshipping the sun and Nicole, who is uber focused on protecting her skin, was making the rounds in a wide-brimmed hat, passing around sun block with a stern warning.

I'm old school on the sun. I'm convinced of our need of its provision of vitamin D and the role that sunlight plays in warding off depression. And I think a touch of color looks healthy. I still partake of small doses for a light, natural tan, while protecting my face. I'm not fair-skinned and I don't permit myself to burn or bake myself to a dark, unnatural shade. I've never used a tanning bed or booth in my life. I'm more suspicious of artificial light.

Jane Gordon was manning the grill, serving up barbecued chicken, and grilled Portobello mushrooms and red peppers for the girls like her, who don't eat meat. She had also made her famous green apple slaw and brought some of June's lemon blueberry cupcakes. The cooler was full of natural sodas and bottled water.

I had invited Jewel to come and Girl Power's director, Sheila Frazier, was explaining to her how the organization works.

"We get referrals from school counselors and meet with the girls' parents or guardians to get their cooperation for the program," Sheila was telling her.

"What are the typical requirements for a referral?" Jewel asked.

"Well, two really. They must demonstrate some sort of creative gift like dancing, drawing, singing or writing. The other is a lack of resources – usually financial, but sometimes the parents are just neglectful. Some of these girls come from very dysfunctional families and we try to get them the counseling they need, in those cases." She pointed to the two women who had helped her carpool the girls to the party. "Kathy and Kim are licensed counselors who assist me with the group. We've had a few girls with some serious issues. We try to refocus them on their gifts. Sometimes we're able to pair them with a mentor, as in the case of Ruby," she smiled at me. "She's taken a real interest in Jordan Kozyra and we cleared it with her mother to let Ruby sponsor private voice and drama lessons for her. This swim party is a rare opportunity to get the girls together in a purely social setting. We're trying to encourage them to bond together as a group and support one another. We really appreciate this, Ruby."

"It's my pleasure," I said. "How is Jordan doing?"

I watched her spiking volleyballs with a few girls over at a net on the side of the lawn. They laughed as Jonah and Ginger chased the ball's progress from one side of the net to the other.

"She missed an audition over in St. Louis last Saturday," Sheila answered. "Her mother was supposed to take her, but she had one of her sick headaches and backed out without telling us. Maybe you could encourage Jordan to call one of us to step in when something like that happens. She tends to keep things locked up inside."

"I'll see what I can do."

"Good," she nodded. "I'm going to circulate. Nice to meet you, Jewel," she said and headed back towards the pool.

"That's Jordan playing volleyball in the green bikini," I told Jewel. "I think I'll go check on her. Do you mind?" I asked.

"Of course not. I'm going to say hello to Jane Gordon."

I joined the girls at the net and volleyed back and forth with them for a few minutes. I had played briefly on a girls' team in high school and could still hold my own. When they took a break to get a soda, I suggested to Jordan that we step inside for a moment. I has some sheet music I wanted to give her for her voice lessons.

"I wasn't sure if you'd have a beach bag, so I put these in a waterproof folder for you," I told her, once we were in the living room. "Show those to your vocal coach. Maybe there's something there you can use for auditions."

"Thank you," she smiled. She hesitated for a moment, then gave me an awkward hug.

"Let's sit down for a minute." I pointed to the sofa and we both plopped down. "Sheila told me you missed an audition last weekend."

Her cheeks flushed with color and she looked down at the floor, saying nothing. I knew that working in a doctor's office meant Jordan's mother had access to free drug samples. Sheila had shared with me that she sometimes self-medicated with pills.

"I want you to know that you don't have to deal with everything alone. Wait here a minute."

I went to my desk in my study and got one of my special business cards with the ruby dagger and took it back to her.

"The next time something like that happens, I want you to contact me and let me talk to your mom to see if I can help you both out, okay?"

"Okay," she smiled. "Thank you." She looked at the card. "That's the ruby dagger from *The Desert Queen*."

"That's right," I nodded. "I only give those cards out to special people. That's my private cell phone number and my private email address."

"I won't share them with anyone, Ruby. I promise."

"I trust you. Now go on back out and join the party."

Her smile was much more relaxed as she headed back out to the pool. Jewel passed her in the doorway and made her way over to me. She sat down across from me and smiled.

"Do some good?" she asked.

"I hope so. She's such a sweet girl. I want to help make sure she gets the opportunity to become everything she wants to be."

"Excuse me." It was one of the middle school girls – a quiet one who mostly kept to herself. "Can I use the restroom?"

"Sure," I told her. "There's a powder room right down this hallway on the right."

"Thank you."

She smiled shyly and headed quickly towards the hall. In her haste, she bumped into an end table and a vase went crashing to the oak floor, breaking into several pieces.

"Oh my God! I'm so sorry." She looked at us with a horrified expression.

"Don't worry about it. It's just a vase. It wasn't from the Ming Dynasty or anything," I joked, hoping to put her at ease.

She bent down to pick up a piece and the sharp edge cut her hand right open. She dropped the pottery and looked at her bleeding hand, mortified. It reminded me of the night I broke the wine pitcher outside.

Jewel had crouched down by the girl and reached out for her hand. "Here, let me see." Then she turned back to me. "Why don't you pick up the pieces and I'll take care of her."

"There's some antiseptic cream in the medicine cabinet in the powder room," I told her.

She nodded and took hold of the girl and led her down the hallway. I picked up the broken pottery and deposited it in the kitchen trash. Then I went outside and rejoined the volleyball game.

The party had been a success and Nicole and I helped load tired girls and their beach bags into the chaperones' cars. The girl who broke the vase offered me a shy smile as she handed me her bag to load into the trunk.

"How is your hand?" I asked her.

"I'm sorry?" she said and shook her head. I reached for her injured hand and turned it over. There was no evidence of a cut and the girl was looking at me in a state of confusion. I felt certain her hand got cut but I didn't want to upset her again.

"No, I'm sorry." I said. "I must have you confused with one of the other girls."

She thanked me for the party and climbed into the car. I spotted Jewel getting into her own car. She smiled and waved before she got behind the wheel. I played the scene back in my mind, wondering if I had misunderstood something, but it didn't really matter, so I shook it off as I watched her drive away.

With the party over, I decided to relax and enjoy some quiet time to myself. I spent the next few days reading, watching movies, and working out in my gym as I contemplated my next book. My life had returned to a normal routine.

It was the calm before the storm.

*****

Chapter 26

Friday evening arrived and I showered and dressed for the charity event. I had attended a costume party that Nicole had hosted the previous year as a flapper girl, and I still had the elements of that outfit – a red lace cocktail dress, silver art deco strappy heels, drop earrings, a long silver art deco style necklace, and a rhinestone headband. I had found the headband in a vintage shop on Cherokee Street in St. Louis. It was a fun piece, and I was glad to get an opportunity to wear it again. I went with dramatic makeup – dark, smoky eyes and dark red lips. I put a few items in a beaded silver clutch and surveyed myself in the mirror. *Not bad.*

Derek arrived in a pin stripe suit, complete with wing tip shoes and a fedora.

"Wow. You look fantastic," he said.

"So do you."

"The fedora is not overkill?"

"No, I think it's hot. I love a guy in a fedora."

"Is that a fact?"

The sexy grin was back, and he pulled me against him, reminiscent of the first time we met, and my pulse did a crazy dance.

"You're going to need to fix your lipstick," he warned right before his mouth came down on mine in our first serious kiss. It was so arousing I had to break it off before I decided to skip the party and lead him upstairs.

He watched with a satisfied smile as I pulled a compact mirror and lipstick out of my clutch and repaired my lips. Then I took a handkerchief and wiped the lipstick off his mouth and told him we should get going.

"Where's Jonah?" he asked on the way out.

"Sleeping over with Ginger," I told him.

"I'm impressed. She's a looker!"

We laughed and made our way to his car as thunder rumbled in the distance.

"Sounds like we're going to get a storm tonight. Hopefully, it will break up this heat wave," he said as he opened the car door for me.

"Well, I love a good thunderstorm," I told him.

"I like them too." He grabbed my hand and kissed the inside of my wrist before he helped me into the car and closed the door.

On the drive over, we talked about our careers, which eventually led to the theater project. I told him about my love of movies and the history of the

Paramount, and how much pleasure it was giving me to restore it.

He told me about the history of the Thaxton Building, where the party was being held, and that it was now listed on the National Register of Historic Places.

When we arrived, he turned the car over to a valet and verified our names on the guest list, then we took a stroll through the building. It was just as stunning as he had described — a multi-level venue with an art deco motif and period artwork covering the walls in colorful frescoes. The main hall was set up with gaming tables and appetizer stands. Upstairs on the mezzanine overlooking the main floor there were poker tables and a small, tasteful bar. The downstairs level was the true speakeasy, with a larger, ornate bar, cozy seating areas, a dance floor and a DJ spinning a nice fusion of swing era, standards, and more contemporary jazz music. There was a capacity crowd. The joint was definitely jumpin'.

There was a photo booth set up under the stairs and Derek suggested we have our picture taken together. He struck a tough guy pose and I draped myself against him and gave my best come hither smile. They gave us both a copy. Derek stashed his copy in his wallet, and I tucked mine into my purse.

He ordered a beer for himself and a signature cherry moonshine cocktail for me before we settled in at one of the Texas Hold'em tables. I decided I was going to have to pace myself with the moonshine. It had a nice kick and went down like Kool-Aid.

On the drive over, I had told him about Max's skill at Hold'em and his desire to turn pro when he completed his economics degree. Derek had said he didn't think that was a bad move if he was really good at it, and he could always turn to something else if it didn't work out. He liked that Max was majoring in economics, just as he had, and suggested that perhaps Max might like to try working in his venture capital business if poker didn't work out for him. My respect for and attraction to this man were growing exponentially.

The hostess had given us vouchers for chips when we checked in. Derek said there were some donated prizes for the high winners of the evening, but the proceeds of the party were going to Stray Rescue, a popular no-kill shelter in St. Louis. As it turned out, he was a decent poker player – better than I was, despite the basic strategy lessons Max had taught me. I held my own through several hands, then went all in on pocket 10s against Derek's Q-9 on a large pot. After the turn and the river, he held trip queens and I was out. I decided to go downstairs and try my hand at blackjack instead.

I'm not big on gambling. I had grown up on the lower end of middle class. We had a decent house and all the necessities of life, but there were no vacations or private lessons or anything of that nature, and I had worn my share of Rachael's hand-me-downs. I had a healthy respect for money, so I tended to be conservative at gaming tables. I played for awhile, holding my own. Eventually the guy next to me turned and offered his hand.

"Mitchell Halliday. I'm Derek's CFO for the St. Louis office."

"Ruby January." I smiled and shook his hand.

"Yes, I know. Derek has talked about you in the office. We're all happy to see him interested in another woman. I guess you know about Melanie?"

I nodded.

"Well, we all liked her, but there comes a time when you have to let go and get on with life. If you really care for him, don't let him get away."

"Thank you." I patted his arm. "I'm going down to the bar. It was nice to meet you."

He nodded and turned back to the game, and I made my way through the crowd to the bar downstairs.

"I'll have another cherry moonshine," I told a female bartender. She was a beautiful young black woman with cocoa skin and shiny dark hair.

"Those are good, aren't they?" she laughed.

"Yes," I laughed back. "I'm trying to pace myself."

"Smart plan."

She set my drink down and turned to another patron.

"She's right. You are smart to pace yourself on those, chica."

It was Ramirez, decked out in gangster finery. I was caught off guard but recovered nicely.

"I don't need your advice, and I'm not your chica."

"So, the claws are out," he said. "Claws can be dangerous, on a woman or an animal."

"Are you admitting you sent that wolf after me? Not too subtle, are you?"

"Subtlety bores the hell out of me. I prefer a direct approach."

The pretty bartender was back. She smiled and asked what she could do for him. He laid his hand on her arm and looked into her eyes for a moment.

"You can unbutton your blouse and show me what you've got under there."

I watched in shock as she smiled slowly and reached for the top button of her blouse.

"Never mind," he laughed. "I'll have a bourbon, neat," he said, and she went to get it.

"You see what I mean?" he said to me. He reached for the ornament at the end of my necklace and stroked it between his fingers. "That's an interesting necklace. Not as interesting as the ruby necklace you described in your novel."

"That's what this is all about, isn't it?" I said to him. "Your trip to this area. You're all searching for a necklace that some crazy old woman told David was buried in some third world country. You're wasting your time. That legend is a work of fiction, just like my novel."

The bartender brought his drink with a smile and he winked at her and downed a healthy slug before he turned back to me.

"Pursuing something of beauty is never a waste of time, chica – whether it be a necklace or a woman. Enjoy your evening."

He sauntered through the crowd and up the stairs and I turned and scanned the room for Angelique. I was pretty sure she had been his entrée to this private party of wealthy locals. I spotted her sitting alone at a small, round cocktail table in a corner. I walked over and sat down without asking permission. She was drinking what appeared to be the apple moonshine cocktail and wearing a white flapper dress with a black feather headband and long, black beads. Her makeup was also dramatic to the era.

"Where's Marco? Did he come with you?" I asked her.

"He's playing chauffeur tonight. He does whatever Rey asks him to do. I believe he's outside smoking with the other chauffeurs."

"Does he have a machine gun stashed in the car, like a proper Prohibition-era thug?" I asked.

She shrugged her shoulders and crunched on some ice from her drink, surveying the room with a bored expression.

"Isn't it time for you all to return to New York, Angie? There are no projects in La Vista for Ramirez to pursue and he is not going to find a ruby necklace here."

"I'm trying to persuade him of that, believe me. He appears to be nearly ready, and I am more than ready. I guess that's something I have in common with my mother. I don't find this area particularly charming."

"Do you find Ramirez charming? He's a sociopath. Why don't you terminate your relationship with him, for your own safety?"

She took a drink and smiled at me. "You know what they say. Keep your friends close and your enemies closer. I like to know what he's up to."

"And do you? Have you discovered if he had something to do with David's disappearance?"

Silence.

"What about Melanie Mayhall? Did he have her abducted and sold into slavery?"

She looked at me caustically. "Do you really care? Doesn't that work to your advantage?"

"Of course I care, Angelique, and surely you do, as well. That's a horrible thing to happen to a woman. That could just as easily be you or me."

"You and I are both gifted, and a lot smarter than Melanie Mayhall. You should forget about her and worry about yourself. As I've said, Rey is not someone to mess around with. You should try to avoid him until he tires of this game and leaves."

She stood and turned to exit, but I reached out and grabbed her arm.

"I saw a vision of you at my house the night of the cocktail party. Was that you trying to reach out to me? Are you in danger from him, Angelique?"

She looked into my eyes for a moment, then pulled her arm free.

"Watch your back," she said and disappeared into the crowd.

After a few minutes I saw Derek making his way towards me, a concerned look on his face.

"There you are." He sat down next to me. "I saw Ramirez upstairs in the poker room. I wanted to make sure you were okay. Was he bothering you?"

"No, I'm fine, Derek. Angelique says they are gearing up to go back to New York."

He nodded. "That's probably for the best. Jack and I have not come up with anything new on him. I'm not sure we ever will."

He looked resigned and I didn't want the shadow of any of those people to spoil our evening together.

"I met Mitch Halliday at the blackjack table," I smiled.

"Oh yeah? Did you thrash him soundly, I hope?" he laughed.

"No, I'm not a big gambler. I came down here to enjoy the music for awhile."

Right on cue, Sarah Vaughan's version of "Misty" started playing.

"Oh, I love this song," I said. "I sang this at Nicole's and Kyle's wedding reception."

"Really?" He looked intrigued. "Let's dance."

He grabbed my hand and led me out onto the floor. Sarah Vaughan's gorgeous alto, interspersed between sexy saxophone riffs, filled the room and I relaxed into his lead. He was a good dancer for a big, muscular guy. Those green eyes were burning into me and I felt my pulse start up again. Green fire and cherry moonshine.

"I'd like to hear you sing sometime," he said in a husky voice.

"I'm a little rusty, but I'll give it a whirl."

I slipped my arms around his neck and sang a verse seductively into his ear.

He pulled back and looked into my eyes again. "Let's get out of here."

He got no argument from me as he took my hand and pulled me up the stairs and out the front door. He stood smiling at me on the sidewalk while the valet went to get the car. I stood there smiling back at him as the wind from the approaching storm whipped my skirt and hair. I didn't let on that I could see Marco Ramirez sitting over on a curb with some other men, smoking, just as Angelique had predicted. If Derek saw him, he didn't let on either.

When the car arrived, the valet took me around to the passenger side while Derek relieved himself of his fedora, jacket and tie, and tossed them onto the back seat. He tipped the valet, rolled up his sleeves and slid inside.

"That's better," he grinned and eased into the traffic on Olive Street. "I like your voice," he said after a moment.

I was quiet for a moment, then I told him about my lost dreams of singing and acting, and how I had turned to writing instead.

"Well, I think that worked out okay for you, didn't it?" he grinned.

"Yes. I believe things worked out the way they were supposed to." I was silent for a moment, then I asked him, "Derek, do you believe in telepathy?"

"What exactly do you mean?"

"I mean seeing things that haven't happened yet in a dream, or sensing something that has happened but no one has told you about – things like that."

"Do you mean like Angelique can do?"

I pulled up in surprise. "You know about that?"

"She told me something once that she had seen in a dream – something she couldn't have known. I think she was trying to impress me. I think everyone experiences things like that once in a while, like déjà vu. But I guess there are some people who have a stronger propensity for it." He looked over at me. "Why are you asking me this? Did *you* see something in a dream?" he smiled.

"Yes." I hesitated for a moment. "You. Before we met."

"Really? What was I doing?"

"I'm not sure. I think you were trying to protect me, or maybe warn me about something. You gave me the ruby necklace from my novel."

I watched for his reaction.

He sighed heavily. "I wish none of us had ever heard of that necklace. It's done nothing but cause trouble for people." He looked over at me. "You're not thinking that I have it, or know where to find it, are you?"

"No," I shook my head. "Are you thinking that I do? Is that why you wanted to get close to me?

Angelique suggested that you might be thinking you could use it to get Melanie back."

He pulled abruptly off the highway, turned on the emergency blinkers and took my face in his hands.

"No. I don't think anyone knows where that necklace is, and I'm not persuaded that it even exists. I was dismayed when you included it in your novel. I worried it might place you in danger, just as it may have done for Melanie and David. But I got close to you because I wanted to."

He kissed me hard and I forgot about everything but him as he started back out onto the highway. When we pulled onto my drive, he got out and walked me to the door. He waited while I disarmed the alarm and tossed my clutch on a table. I turned back to him and he pulled me into his arms and kissed me again. My head was swimming as he backed me against the wall and I instinctively ground my hips into his.

He caught his breath and pulled back from me. I could see the turmoil on his face, and I knew why it was there. There was something real between us and, if he slept with me, he would be letting go of Melanie. I didn't want her ghost in bed with us. He was too important to me, and I wanted him to be certain.

"Maybe we should dial this back a notch, until we're both sure," I said raggedly.

I watched desire war with reason on his face and then he nodded, kissed me again and told me he would call me. I let him go. Then I walked back outside, dropping my shoes on the patio as I headed out into the back yard where the wind was whipping the tree limbs around and thunder cracked loudly over the river. I moved my bare feet sensuously through the grass and swayed into the breeze, dancing across the lawn in a primordial sexual rhythm, oblivious to anything but my physical senses. As I swirled around, I caught a glimpse of white out of the corner of my eye. It was Derek's shirt. He stood on the patio watching me, transfixed, then he started towards me with a steady purpose.

I stood there heaving in anticipation until he hauled me against him and his mouth came down on mine. I wrapped my legs around his waist as he turned in sensuous circles and then pulled me down onto the ground on top of him. I took off the long necklace and tossed it into the grass, then pulled my dress over my head. He rolled over on top of me, ripping at his shirt buttons. I helped him get them open and he stood and pulled off the rest of his clothes. He was the epitome of masculinity standing there in the elements with lightning flashing in the background. I reached out for him and he came down on top of me.

I didn't care that we were naked in the open or that I was wearing a rhinestone headband. In a moment like that, everything fades in deference to the elemental relationship between a man and a woman and I followed his wild rhythm as thunder and lightning echoed around us. I heard myself calling out his name, and then I melted into a limp pool of dark satisfaction.

Eventually, I became aware of the weight of him on me, his sweaty chest heaving back into a slower rhythm. And then the raindrops started and we laughingly struggled to our feet, grabbing our clothes up out of the grass, and ran naked across my lawn to the safety of the house, just as the skies opened up. He carried me upstairs and I directed him to my room, where we fell onto my bed in an exhausted tangle of limbs as the storm raged outside.

That's the last thing I remember before I fell into the most satisfying sleep of my life.

✶✶✶✶✶

Chapter 27

The next morning, I woke up and realized I was alone in the bed. I rolled over and found a yellow hibiscus bloom on the other pillow. He had obviously picked it off one of the bushes on my patio. Yellow is my favorite.

I wondered if he was gone, but a quick look around revealed our clothes piled neatly on a chaise. I hauled myself out of bed and pulled on a fresh pair of panties and a long, white v-neck tee, then made my way into the bathroom, where I washed my face, brushed my teeth and ran a comb through my hair. I noticed that he had found my stash of new toothbrushes and made use of one. I was pleased that he was making himself at home. Then I tucked his flower behind my ear and made my way downstairs.

There was a faint clanging of metal and I followed it to my gym and found him doing bench presses in nothing but his boxers. I caught my breath and took in that sight silently for a moment. I had installed the bench press for Max. He enjoyed using it when he was home, but I was the one enjoying it now. Derek obviously worked out on a regular basis and still had the physique of a Navy

Seal. After a moment he noticed me, and he sat up and grinned.

"Good morning."

"Hi there," I said and walked over and straddled the bench in front of him.

He smiled at the flower in my hair and bent to kiss me. We sat there looking at one another for a moment. I traced the scar on his cheek with my finger. "How did you get that?"

"Knife fight in Syria."

"I hope the other guy looks worse."

"The other guy is dead," he said matter-of-factly.

"Oh. Well done, then, I guess."

He just nodded and I searched his face for any sign of regret over what had happened between us, but didn't see any.

"Are you hungry?" I asked him.

"Starving."

"How about pancakes? I've got real Vermont maple syrup."

"Sounds good."

"I can't function without my iced tea. I don't drink coffee, but I keep it around for Max. He occasionally has a cup in the morning. Would you rather have that?"

"I only drink coffee when it's cold outside. I'd rather have orange juice, if you've got it. If not, iced tea is fine."

"I've got it. You finish your workout."

I fixed the pancakes and set up in the breakfast nook. The storm had indeed cooled things off and I opened the windows to let in the fresh breeze. He told me he had a meeting with Halliday and a client in St. Louis and couldn't stay much longer. I offered him my shower and we ended up in there together and made love again.

He promised to call me later and when he left I got dressed and headed over to Nicole's to fetch Jonah. I rolled down the car windows and enjoyed a leisurely drive. I couldn't ever remember feeling so happy. It must have shown because Nicole took one look at my face and laughed.

"Looks like Ginger isn't the only girl who had a sleepover."

I just grinned and flopped down on her couch to pet the dogs.

"What about you? Have you heard from Jack?"

"He called and we talked for awhile. I'm taking that slowly. I'll probably go over there and shoot with him again sometime soon," she smiled.

I nodded and returned her smile. "What are you going to do today?" I asked her.

"I don't know. I might head up to Grafton and spend some time with my parents. I was hoping we might do a walk-through with Jamie today to get a final punch list for the subcontractors to complete, but he can't make it."

"He has more pressing plans than our project?" I teased, still in my haze of pleasure.

"He's too distracted today, I think. He said his daughter didn't come home last night."

I sat up straight as my heart slammed into my gut.

"What do you mean?"

She shrugged. "She worked a shift at The Loading Dock last night, and then never came home afterward. And she's not answering her cell phone. He found her car still in the parking lot. She got off at 11:00 last night and no one has talked to her since. Hey, she's what, 18 years old? She probably just passed out at a friend's house. You remember how it is at that age." She sat down and got a good look at my face. "What's wrong?"

"In one of the dreams that I've had lately, Meryl Sinclair was in some kind of trouble. She was running down a hiking trail in Grafton. I got the feeling it had something to do with Ramirez."

"Seriously?" Nicole knew from our childhood that my dreams sometimes predicted something real. I had shared that much with her back then. "Well, maybe it's just a coincidence, or maybe it meant something else. Nothing is certain yet. It could be like I said and she's just sleeping off a night of partying somewhere."

"Maybe. Did he call the police?"

"He talked to a friend on the force, but she's of legal age and there's no evidence of foul play, so she can't be reported missing until 24 hours have passed. They're hoping she is just sleeping somewhere, but you know he's a real worrywart when it comes to her."

I nodded. "Well, if you hear anything at all, will you let me know? I just want to know that she's okay."

"Will do. And you do the same, okay?"

I agreed and collected Jonah and headed back home. I thought about Rey and Marco being at the party last night and how that gave them an alibi, but maybe they had planned it that way. I hoped I was being overly dramatic, but my instincts told me I wasn't. I knew I wasn't going to be able to relax until I knew for sure, so I dropped Jonah off at home and headed towards Grafton. It was a beautiful day for a drive up the River Road, but my happy mood was gone with the wind.

*****

Chapter 28

When I reached Grafton, I followed my instincts and pulled into the Wind Rivers Condos. Once again, I drove slowly through the complex, hoping to spot Angelique's car; once again, to no avail. But as I was heading for the gate, I spotted her over by the private pool. I parked and made my way over to her. She was sunning herself in a red bikini. The only other person around was a young guy sprawled in a lounger across the pool. He was doing his best to pretend his eyes were closed, but he was really watching her through the slits. I dropped down on the lounge chair next to her.

"I've got some extra suits if you want to work on your tan," she said.

"No thanks. This isn't a social call."

She sighed, sat up and reached for her water bottle. "I didn't believe for a moment that it was."

"How late were you at the party last night?" I asked her.

"What difference does it make?"

"I want to know Ramirez's whereabouts. Jamie Sinclair's daughter didn't come home last night."

"What does that have to do with Rey?"

"Hopefully, nothing. But I had a dream that suggests otherwise, and we both know how telling a dream can be."

She watched me silently for a moment. "We stayed until the party was nearly over – close to midnight. He seemed to be enjoying himself and was reluctant to leave. Marco was there the whole time, as well. There are other chauffeurs who can attest to that."

"That's all just a little too tidy, don't you think?"

"What I think is that you need to heed my warnings and keep your distance from Rey. He's starting to make plans to leave this area and return to New York. If there is any foul play involving the Sinclair girl, I'm sure the authorities will investigate."

"Like they investigated Melanie Mayhall's disappearance? We both know how that turned out."

"If it will make you feel any better, I'll have a look around up there and see what I can find out."

I searched in my purse and pulled out one of my cards with the ruby dagger on it. "Here's my cell number if you need to contact me."

She glanced at the card and gave me a sardonic look. "Sure. I'll let you know if I run across that stupid necklace, while I'm at it."

"Just be careful, Angelique. I'm sure you're smart enough not to openly challenge him. Heed your own advice and exercise some caution."

I got up and made my way around the pool. She watched me leave and the young guy took advantage of the situation and executed a dive into the deep end, hoping to impress her. Unfortunately, he belly-flopped. I hoped that wasn't an omen of things to come.

*****

Chapter 29

The next stop on my list was The Loading Dock. I pulled into the parking lot, where Meryl's Passat was parked next to a tree. The lunch crowd was starting to filter in, so I waited until I was alone in the lot before I got out and took a peek in her car. There was not much to see, except that she was a slightly messy person who left clutter in the seats and floorboards of her car – a pet peeve of mine. On the other hand, Jamie had already been there, so he could have removed anything important, like her purse, if it had been there.

My next stop was the lot at St. Patrick's. Staring up at the bluff house from this vantage point was getting old, but I didn't know what else to do at that point. I cleared my mind and concentrated on the bedroom in the back hallway, and the feeling of raw fear came over me in a rush. I felt certain that meant she was up there.

"Excuse me. Are you the florist?"

I'd been so absorbed I hadn't noticed the woman approaching. "I'm sorry?"

"Are you here to set up for the wedding this evening?"

"Oh. No. Sorry."

"Oh, no problem," she laughed. "Sorry for the mistake."

I got back in my car and started formulating a plan. The police could not help until 11:00 that night, but she might be gone by then. I wondered if I should call Derek, but I kept remembering the dream and how I had been running behind the young woman, and he pulled me off the path and seemed to thwart my efforts. I believed that was not only a premonition, but also some kind of directive. Maybe if Derek got involved something would go wrong.

I decided I needed Nicole's help and took a drive by her parents' house. Her car was there. I stopped and knocked on the door.

"Hey, kid. Come on in. You looking for Nic?"

It was Nicole's father. He looked much the same as he had when I really was a kid - tall with steel-gray hair and piercing blue eyes, but a slight paunch had settled around his mid-section in his retirement.

"Hi Lee."

Nicole appeared behind him.

"What's up?" she grinned. "You want to join us for lunch? Mom had a special order and couldn't get away from the market."

"I need to talk to you about something."

"I'll just take the dogs out for a walk," Lee said, politely. He put Ginger and his chow on leashes and slipped out the door.

Nicole and I sat down on the porch swing and I shared with her the relevant part of the dream and that I believed Meryl was being held in the Ramirez house. I wanted her to know what I was planning to do, in case something went wrong, but I also needed her help with something.

"Can you get me the floor plans for that house?" Her eyes widened. "Doesn't that young guy in the building inspector's office have a crush on you?"

"Yes," she nodded. "That's not ethical, but I'm sure I can persuade him."

She reached him on the phone and told him she recently attended a party there and wanted to see a detail on something for a house plan she was working on. He was thrilled to be able to help her and promised to email them pronto, and not to tell anyone.

Nicole got off the phone and rolled her eyes. "He's going to be a pain in my ass now. I hope this helps."

"Me too. I need to scope out that trail. It doesn't look like the storm hit very hard up here last night."

"No. Dad said it rained lightly for a little while, and that was about it. Nothing like we got."

"Want to take a ride on your dirt bike?"

We rode up the steep hill to Aeries Winery, where I knew an entrance onto the path behind the parking lot. The path was not suitable for a heavy street bike, like Jamie's, but it was fine for a dirt bike, and it was already drying up from the brief rain. We took the trail slowly, at the speed of a person running. I paid close attention to the length and width, and watched for any potentially precarious sections. We pulled up when we were close to the Ramirez house and I sat there pondering how to pull it off.

"If I could just be sure Rey wasn't in the house, I feel confident I could handle Marco. But Rey is a different ballgame."

I wasn't ready to tell Nicole or anyone else all of the secrets I had learned. A part of me understood Jewel's private nature on the subject. Some things aren't meant to be shared with others. But I did tell her about his hypnotic ability and how he must have done that to her that day on the boardwalk. That made her angry. She turned around and I recognized the look in her eyes.

"I can lure Rey out of the house for you."

"No way," I shook my head. "He's too dangerous."

"No, listen. I'll meet him in a public place where he can't do anything to me. How about The Loading Dock? There's poetic justice in that. I'll tell him I've changed my mind about working with him and want to propose a project. I'll make sure to stay in the middle of the crowd."

"What if he doesn't bite?"

"Then I'll sweeten the pot. I'll hint that I know something about that necklace."

"I don't know, Nic. Even in public, it's dangerous."

"Okay, I'll tell my dad this guy is a jerk and I don't trust him. He'll be happy to sit at a nearby table and keep an eye on me. You know how protective he is. And I'll definitely have my gun in my purse."

I nodded. "Okay, if you're sure. That should give me enough time, I think. Just don't let him touch you. I know that sounds crazy."

"It doesn't matter how crazy it sounds. He already did it to me once, and this gives me the chance to pay him back." She looked back towards the house again. "If she is in there, how can you be sure he won't move her before dark?"

"It's not going to happen that way. You'll have to trust me on that."

We rode back to her parents' house and disappeared into the den while her dad whipped up some lunch for us. The floor plans were in her email and we studied them together, looking at the entrance and egress locations, and the windows at the back of the house.

"How do you plan on dealing with the alarm system? I remember seeing a code panel by the front door," she said.

"I'm hoping to find a window open, or a door. Maybe it won't be set yet for the night. I'll figure something out. I just need you to send me a text when you see Ramirez at The Loading Dock. But don't let him see you do it."

"Okay." She hesitated a moment, then asked, "Are you sure you don't want to ask Derek for help on this? He knows these people and he was special forces. He was trained to deal with situations like this."

"This is not a normal situation, and I have a better chance if I do this on my own. We'll set a deadline for you to hear from me. If you haven't, you can call Derek and let him decide how to handle it. I'll give you his cell number. Why don't you call Jamie now and check to see if he's heard anything, just to make sure."

"All right," she agreed.

She called his cell and told him she was concerned and wanted to make sure Meryl had come home. He told her they still hadn't found her and she didn't answer her cell. He promised to let Nicole know when he'd found her.

"He sounded so distraught," she told me. "I'm beginning to believe you're right about this whole thing."

"I hope I'm not, but you should call Ramirez now."

He had given her his business card when they met and I listened as she made her invitation.

"Yes, I know, but it's a woman's prerogative to change her mind, right?" She shook her head at me. "I was interested in doing a project with you, but was reluctant because of Ruby. She has some irrational suspicion towards you." She paused for a second. "I think she's got a secret she's trying to protect and I don't want to alarm her."

"Nice touch," I told her when she got off the phone.

"He wasn't really biting at first, but mentioning your secret sealed the deal."

We made our final plans and did our best to behave normally while we ate lunch with her dad. Then he walked me to my car.

"You give me a call if this foreign buggy leaves you high and dry on the highway," he advised me in a teasing tone.

"You'll be the first person I call," I laughed back.

I headed back down the River Road, longing for the days when car trouble was the worst thing I had to worry about.

*****

Chapter 30

There were only a few cars on the parking lot at Aeries, as it was early yet for a Saturday night. Even so, I parked at the back of the lot, near the brush that hid the trail. My hair was pulled back with a dark headband and I was dressed in a black tee shirt, dark-wash jeans and black running shoes. My knife sheath was strapped onto my belt, and my Beretta was tucked into a snug thigh holster right below it. I sent a text to let Nicole know I was starting down the path, then I set my phone to vibrate mode and tucked it and my car remote into the pockets of my jeans.

Moonlight broke through the canopy of trees along the trail, faint but enough for me to find my way. It would be easy to succumb to fear in this situation, but I had taught myself at an early age to distract my thoughts to counter fear, and I was thinking about my mother as I made my way steadily along the deserted path. I understood why she had been so agitated when I told her about my dreams.

It was one in which I had seen her with a handsome man, whom I knew now to be my real father. Her reaction had been so negative that I had repressed the dream into some dark corner of my mind. I had only recently recalled it and recognized the man as David Vaughn. I'm sure she was not only frightened by my ability to tap into hidden knowledge, but also afraid her embarrassing secret would emerge. She must have wondered if telling him when she first found out would have made any difference, since it had for Cassandra, but she probably also suffered from self-doubts about her socioeconomic background, just as I had when Jamie chose Elizabeth Hayden over me. Perhaps my mother even feared she would lose me over her deception.

I understood her pain and I was no longer angry with her over her choices in life. She did the best that she knew how to do and that was all there was to it. Most of us try to do the best we can with what we've been given to work with. I had inherited some of my mother's good qualities, like her love of animals and her penchant for daily walks on nature trails. We both loved stained glass, and I hung wind chimes on my balcony because they reminded me of her. My mother always kept wind chimes outside of her windows. I hoped she had enjoyed some measure of happiness with my stepdad. He was a nice man and she and David were probably not well-suited for a long-term relationship. I hoped she had not wasted too much emotion pining away for him, as I had Jamie. I was now hoping for a future with Derek.

Just as I thought of him, my phone vibrated. I assumed it was Nicole, but when I pulled the phone out of my pocket, it was Derek's name on the readout. I held my breath as I stood there on the trail letting the phone continue to vibrate. There was no way I was going to talk to him before I had completed my mission. I didn't want to lie to him and he would be furious if he knew what I was doing. But he didn't know all of the mitigating circumstances, and I didn't want any interference. Still, I felt a sharp twinge of guilt as the call went to voicemail. I tucked the phone back into my pocket and continued on resolutely.

I had reached the section of the path that passed behind the Ramirez house and I took up a position in the brush and waited for Nicole to send the text she had drafted and ready. It seemed like a lifetime, but it was only a few minutes later when it came. Rey was at The Loading Dock, and I relaxed a little and scoped out the house.

I was hoping to spot an open window around the side or back somewhere, but no such luck. I knew from the floor plans that there was a small patio around the back – a different one than the side patio utilized at the cocktail party, and I made my way farther down the path, then dropped down in surprise. There was a man standing right outside the door, smoking a cigarette. It wasn't Marco Ramirez. He looked bored and it appeared that he might be standing guard at the door, as he was wearing a shoulder holster with a handgun tucked into it. That was the bad news. The good news was that the door behind him was open, which also meant the alarm system wasn't activated.

I searched the ground around me and came up with a couple of large pebbles. I lobbed one overhead, aiming at the brush on the other side of the patio. When it hit the mark, he stood there looking around for a moment, then took the bait and headed over to investigate. I held my breath and made my way quickly to some flowering bushes at the side of the patio, then I threw the other pebble farther back into the brush. He disappeared and I made my way to the door and peeked in. There was no one in sight and I slipped inside and quickly got my bearings.

This was the hallway Derek had emerged from on the other side of the bedroom I had been searching. I made my way quietly forward. When I reached the room, I glanced down both directions. There was no one around and I pressed my ear to the door. I heard nothing, but felt the familiar rush of fear come over me.

I pulled my Beretta out of the holster and clicked off the safety in case someone was waiting. The door swung freely open and there appeared to be no one in the room... except for a woman tied to the bed with a gag in her mouth, her long, blonde hair streaming across the pillow. I eased the door shut behind me and moved towards the bed, where I pulled up in shock. It wasn't Meryl Sinclair lying there. It was Angelique. I holstered the gun and reached for the cloth that was tied over her mouth.

"You were right," she whispered. "They have the Sinclair girl in a secret room off the den down the hall. I found her, but Marco followed me back there and caught me by surprise. He hit me so hard I blacked out. When I woke up, I was tied to this bed."

I hesitated for a moment and she sighed in frustration.

"You're going to have to trust me, Ruby. I'm not a paragon of virtue but I wouldn't participate in selling a girl into the sex trade."

I looked more closely at her face. There was a faint red mark on her jaw. I decided to believe her and cut her free.

She rubbed her wrists and sat up. "I came up here under the guise of discussing some business with Rey. I got suspicious when he had extra men in the house, so I excused myself to use the bathroom and slipped into the den. I knew about the secret room from the owner." She caught my questioning look and shrugged her shoulders. "He's an attorney

I'm acquainted with. I slept with him a couple of times. Men will tell you their secrets in bed. He used it to store valuables but moved them out of the house when he started leasing it out. I had shown it to Rey, thinking he might want to store some valuables. I found her bound and gagged on a mattress in there. She was trying to warn me. I turned around just in time to get a glimpse of Marco before he decked me."

"Rey is not in the house right now," I told her, "but we can assume Marco is. I saw a guard outside the back door. Do you know how many more?"

"I think there are three - one at each entrance. How did you get in?"

I told her about the trail.

"Well, let's get the girl before Rey comes back," she suggested. "We'll have to go out a window. Keep your gun ready."

I pulled it back out of the holster as she cracked open the door, took a peek and motioned me to follow her. We moved silently down the hallway I had traveled the night of the cocktail party. She paused in front of a door and peeked inside, then motioned me to follow her in. She closed the door behind me and moved behind a desk at the side of the room, searching for something behind a credenza. She apparently found it, because a bookcase on the far wall swung open. That certainly hadn't been in the floor plans.

She led the way into the hidden room, which wasn't much bigger than an oversized walk-in closet. There was an overhead light and a vent to circulate the air conditioning, but there was nothing else inside except a mattress where Meryl Sinclair was indeed bound and gagged, dressed in shorts, tennis shoes and a tank top. She looked exhausted and terrified. Her eyes widened when I pulled out my dagger.

"It's okay," I told her. "I'm just cutting you loose." I worked on her bonds while Angelique pulled off her gag and warned her to be quiet.

"Are you all right?" she whispered to Angelique. "He hit you so hard."

"I'm okay. Come on, let's get you up."

We both helped pull her to her feet and she looked at me with wide eyes.

"Ruby? What are you doing here?"

"We're going to get you out of here. C'mon."

Angelique moved over to the credenza and hit the button to close the secret door, while I checked out a window at the back of the room.

"This window looks good. It's fairly close to the trail and there are no lights back here."

"Okay, good," Angelique said. "You go ahead. I have to take care of something here."

"What? No, are you crazy? You can't stay here."

"My mother is in this house," she said. "I heard her voice when I was checking for the girl. She was arguing with Marco in a bedroom down the hall. I didn't know she had returned, but for whatever reason she did, I can't leave her here. She's out of her league with them."

I hesitated, trying to figure out what to do.

"I'm not going to argue with you," she said. "You came here for the girl. Now get her to safety." She nodded at me and then moved quickly to the door and disappeared into the hallway, closing the door behind her.

I scoped out the window again and saw the guard from the back door making a casual sweep of the area. I cursed his timing and told Meryl we would have to wait for him to leave. We ducked down beneath the window, out of sight. She looked overwhelmed and I hoped she was up to a mad run down the trail.

"Did they hurt you, Meryl?" I squeezed her arm.

She looked at me, shaking with emotion. "They were going to rape me, weren't they?"

I shook my head. "No, I think they were going to sell you to someone."

She looked horrified and I realized what a sheltered life she had probably lived with her doting parents, private schools and chaperoned vacations.

"There are some bad people in this world, Meryl, and a girl as pretty as you is going to have to be extra careful. Where did they get you? On the parking lot at The Loading Dock?"

"No, it was a woman."

"A woman?" I said, surprised.

"Yes. A customer who had been talking to me about my career plans. I ran into her again on the parking lot when I finished my shift. She said she knew an agent who could get me some modeling gigs and that she had one of his business cards in her car. I followed her to the back of the lot and the last thing I remember was someone grabbing me from behind and putting something over my mouth. I think they drugged me, and then I woke up in here. I was so scared."

I nodded, squeezing her arm reassuringly. I glanced over at the door. Everything was quiet and the guard outside had moved out of sight.

"Okay, listen to me. My car is in the parking lot at Aeries Winery. We're going to run down this trail until we reach it. If you get separated from me, you keep running, as fast as you can. You'll see the lights from the parking lot and if we get separated, you run inside and call the police, okay?"

She nodded and I took one more look outside and slipped the window open. I helped her drop over the sill, then followed her. There was no one in sight and I grabbed her hand and pulled her across the lawn into the woods and onto the trail. I pushed her ahead of me and we broke into a run.

The moon was still bathing the trail with just enough light to see and I realized I was struggling to keep up with her, just like in my dream. She was twenty years younger and, though I was in good shape, I had never been a runner. Then I heard a sound behind me and turned to see a man giving chase.

"Run, Meryl, run!" I called and she kicked into an even higher gear, and I started falling behind her.

She was pulling farther ahead. Pure adrenaline kept me reaching to catch up to her, but I could hear the man gaining on me from behind. I made a bold decision and turned abruptly, running towards him. I launched myself into the air, landing a kick square on his chest. I caught him totally off-guard. Men expect women to run, not go on the attack. He landed on his back with a thud and I was regaining my balance and formulating my next move when I saw a second man approaching at a fast clip. I had some solid self-defense training and could maybe hold my own with one man, but there was no way I could take on two. I elected to turn and run. A large shape emerged from the brush, moving past me in a dark blur.

"Keep running!"

I recognized Derek's voice, and I came to a halt and turned to see him charging the first man in line. He had caught him as he was still trying to reorient himself from my attack and made quick work of him with a vicious blow to the throat. Then he took the man's head in his arms and twisted. The man fell to the ground and I realized Derek had snapped his neck. Even before the man hit the ground, Derek had spun around and dropped to the ground, kicking the second man's legs out from under him as he came into play. The second man was as big as Derek and the two of them rolled across the trail, trading punches and kicks. I saw a glint of steel and realized one of them had pulled a knife and they were fighting for control of it.

Then my attention was caught by a third man running up to the scene. He had a gun in his hand. He was watching them fight and looking for an opportunity to shoot. He paid no attention to me and I reached for the gun in my thigh holster, then changed my mind. It was dark and I didn't want to risk hitting Derek by mistake.

I reached instead for the weapon I was more comfortable with – my dagger. I pulled back into throwing position, just as Derek got the best of his opponent and sank the knife into his chest. I saw the third man taking aim and threw the dagger just as Chase had taught me, envisioning myself hitting my target and following through with my arm. It hit the mark - right where his heart should be. I saw the surprised look on his face as the gun dropped out of his hand and he sank to the ground. Derek shot me a quick look and then went to check out the body.

"Is he dead?" I asked.

Derek pulled my dagger out of him and wiped the blood off on the man's shirt. He came over to me and took my chin in his hand, forcing my eyes up to his.

"Yes, he's dead. They're all dead. Are you all right?"

I nodded and he pulled me into his arms and held me tight for a moment, then pulled back to look at me again.

"I told you to keep running. What the hell were you thinking coming here by yourself?"

I took a good look at him. He was dressed in camouflage pants and a dark tee shirt, and had weapon holsters of his own strapped on. I took my blade from him and holstered it.

"How did you find me?"

"I was in town with Jack. We were staking out Ramirez. Jack is down at The Loading Dock watching over Nicole from a distance. What is she doing alone with him?"

"She's not alone. Her father is nearby watching her. He's an ex-Marine," I added, thinking he would appreciate that. "How did you find me?" I repeated.

"I put a tracker on your car."

"What?"

"Ramirez said something to me at the casino party — something that made me worry for your safety. He was taunting me about Melanie and suggesting that I should try to do a better job of protecting you. I took him seriously. He's a sociopath. So I put a tracker on your car. When I saw that you were up here and Nicole was with Ramirez, I came up and took a look around and figured it out. I was aware of this trail. Jack and I had scoped out the area around that house."

"They were holding a young girl I know — Meryl, the girl who was ahead of me," I told him. "I have to get to her and make sure she's all right."

"You just killed a man. Are *you* all right?"

I nodded. "I'm okay, Derek." I felt strangely calm about the whole thing, like I had known something like this would happen eventually.

"Listen to me. You can't be involved in this." He gestured to the bodies.

"I'm already involved in this."

"But no one knows that. Jack and I can use our connections to clean this up. No one needs to know."

"Meryl has probably contacted the police by now."

"It doesn't matter. You can't be connected to what just happened here on this trail. Do you understand?"

I nodded, but I wasn't sure if that was really possible.

"Derek, Angelique is still back at the house. We've got to go check on her. Marco might still be there."

"Angelique can take care of herself, especially with the Ramirezes."

"No, she helped us. She's in danger there."

He took my face in his hands and I heard the bells of St. Patrick's start ringing. The wedding must have ended.

"Go back to your car. I'm going to hide the bodies and make sure no one else follows. The police will check on Angelique when they go to find Ramirez. I need you somewhere safe." He hauled me against him once more and whispered in my ear, "I can't lose you too, Ruby."

I pulled back and looked at him as the bells continued their glad tidings and the last piece of the dream fell into place. He hadn't been able to save Melanie and he wasn't going to fail again. I saw the desperation in his eyes and nodded my compliance. I gave him a quick kiss and headed back down the trail at a jog.

When I reached the parking lot, I cut through the trees to my car and got another surprise. Jewel was leaning against it. Her car was parked next to mine.

"Jewel...what are you doing here?"

"Waiting for you," she smiled faintly.

"I don't understand. Where is the girl – Meryl? Is she inside?"

She shook her head and pointed to her car. I walked over and looked in. Meryl was lying on the back seat. She appeared to be unconscious.

"What happened? Is she hurt?"

"No, she's fine. She's just asleep."

"Asleep?" I said, confused. "Well, did one of you call the police?"

She shook her head. "I'm going to see that she is safely discovered. It will look like she was drugged to steal her purse and left hidden in some bushes. When she wakes up, she won't remember where she's been or who she has seen."

"How can you be sure of that?"

"You'll just have to trust me on that. But you can't be connected to this, not only because of your career, but because of your gifts. You need to keep that part of yourself as private as possible."

I stood looking at her silently for a moment.

"You are at a crossroad, Ruby. Your pursuit of the truth has brought you to it. You want to know what happened to your father, right?" she asked.

I drew a deep breath. "Yes."

She nodded. "That's why I came back to this area – to help you come to terms with who you are and what has happened. You're going back for Angelique, aren't you?"

"Yes," I nodded.

She stepped forward and put her hand on my cheek.

"Remember what you said to me about the dark whispering to you, as well as the light. Be careful about the choices you make tonight. Make sure they are choices you can live with."

Then she turned and made her way to her car, got in and drove away.

*****

Chapter 31

I stood contemplating the trail. I couldn't use it, because of Derek. I could just drive up to the house, but that would eliminate the element of surprise and Derek was tracking my car. I knew it would be best for me to deal with Ramirez without him.

Jewel was right. I was at a crossroad. I unlocked my car, unfastened the gun holster on my thigh and locked it in the concealed carry case in the console. In a moment of crisis on the trail, I had used the weapon that suited who I was — the dagger. I was not going to need a gun anyway — not against Ramirez, and it would be better if I did not carry one into this situation and complicate matters.

I could try to deviate from the trail to get around Derek, but that was risky, and there was another way that would be much faster and would definitely get me past him. I just wasn't sure if I could access it.

I took the steps on the other side of the winery deck. It was deserted on that side of the building as I scoped out the entrance to the zip line. It was naturally closed after dark, but there appeared to be someone still working inside the office. The gate was unlocked and I slipped inside and closed it behind me. I moved silently around the structure to the launch platform at the rear, located a pulley on the cable, and brought it down into position.

I knew from the ride I had taken once that this first leg ended well beyond the Ramirez house. I didn't want to go that far, but I also wasn't going to jump off into the woods in the dark and risk breaking bones. I recalled that there was a clearing on the ride where the line dipped fairly low to the ground briefly and I remember thinking it would be the logical spot to drop off if you were too scared to continue. I was going to make use of it.

I took a deep breath and launched off the platform. The darkness was helpful in more ways than one. It not only hid me from view, it also hid the view from me. It was better not to see how high up I was, which in some spots was frighteningly high. I tried to enjoy the sensation of flying, but I was assailed with vivid flashes of pictures in my mind – Rachael falling from the bluff past the fearsome graphic of the Piasa Bird, my stepfather watching me drive away from the house he shared with my mother the last time I saw him alive, then Angelique taking one last glance at me before she slipped into the hallway alone. I willed the pulley to move faster.

The zip line was on the upper side of the foot trail and I took note of passing the section where I believed Derek was located. The pulley made only a faint whirring noise that I hoped was not detectable from his location. I knew the clearing would be coming up shortly when I realized the line was dipping closer to the ground. I strained to see in the faint moonlight and the clearing came abruptly into view as I passed over some treetops. I waited until I believed I was at the lowest point, then let go and held my breath as the ground rushed up to meet me.

My feet hit the earth in a jarring rush, and I tried to drop naturally and roll to absorb some of the impact. Still, it damn near knocked the wind out of me, and I took a moment to collect myself and make sure I wasn't injured. I quickly got my bearings, made my way into the brush and located the trail. I calculated I was slightly past the house and headed back in that direction.

I made my way along the lonely path in a night gone eerily quiet after the bells of St. Patrick's had concluded their announcement. Along the way, I got a text from Nicole warning me that Ramirez had left and might be headed back to the house. But the warning wasn't necessary. I already knew he was there. I could feel him.

I was back at the same spot I had approached from earlier, at the rear patio. There was no guard to contend with this time and I was moving towards the back door when I heard the faint strains of guitar music. It was coming from the side of the house, from the patio where I had spoken with Ramirez at the cocktail party. I followed the music, transfixed, because I recognized the song.

He was sitting on the same bench where we had conversed, softly plucking out the tune on an acoustic guitar, and he smiled at me and set the instrument aside as I approached.

"There you are, chica. I've been waiting for you. Did you recognize the song?"

"'Little Wildwood Church'," I said.

"Yes. Not to be confused with "The Church in the Wildwood," which is a much more popular tune. I researched it on the internet."

He gestured to the bench and I sat down beside him.

"Most people are not familiar with this song," he continued. "Where did you hear it?"

"My father used to play it on his steel guitar on our back porch. It was the song I first learned to play chords on."

"But he was not your father, was he?"

"No, but I believed he was, and that was all that mattered then."

"It must have been hard growing up with a man like that for a father, then learning you were cheated out of having a man like David Vaughn raise you. Your life could have been very different."

I shrugged. "Probably no harder than being abandoned by your real father. Mine didn't know I existed. Yours rejected you. Do you know who he was?"

"Yes," he nodded. "I eventually discovered his identity. He was an upper class white man and my mother was a poor Mexican girl – very beautiful, but poor and uneducated. She was not a suitable partner for a man like him to marry or even publicly acknowledge, so when she became pregnant, he left her high and dry." He laughed softly. "That might work for a woman of Cassandra's social class, but not for my mother. There were other wealthy men who succumbed to her beauty over the years, but she was not able to land any of them either. They all just used her for pleasure and tossed her aside, and she never learned a damned thing. She just kept repeating the same mistake. She was a weak woman, and her weakness kept us in poverty." He shrugged. "We all have our sob stories, no?"

"So you're getting even with your mother by selling women into the sex trade? Isn't that misguided? It was your father who abandoned you."

"I hope you're not going to start quoting Freud."

"Not me," I shook my head. "Freud was a cokehead and a mama's boy. He did get a few things right. His theory that some of his female patients were suffering emotional problems from being sexualized by male relatives at a young age was right on the money. Too bad he changed his tune when the wealthy Victorian-era husbands and fathers of those women objected."

"That's just good business, Ruby. They were the ones paying his bills. You don't bite the hand that feeds you."

"Do you bite the hand that works for you? Where is Angelique?"

"Where is Angelique," he repeated. "We both have our questions to ask, don't we? Do you know how I first discovered my special abilities?"

He reached into his pocket and produced a pack of matches, lit one and tossed it into the stone pit in front of us, where a fire had been laid out. The wood must have been soaked in lighter fluid because it blazed up immediately. Orange flames crackled and danced in front us.

"Fire is hypnotic," he continued. "I would stare into it and conjure visual images. Eventually I learned how to manipulate the images and be transported into them. I'm curious. Did you also discover the power of fire?"

I watched the flames dancing and saw no reason to lie.

"Yes," I nodded. "There was a barrel in our back yard where my father would burn the trash and my mother would find me staring into it, rocking back and forth like I was in a trance. It frightened her. She took me to a doctor and he sent me to a hospital for an EEG."

"Did they find anything unusual?" he asked.

"No. Nothing."

"I'm not surprised," he shrugged. "Our gifts are not derived from natural sources and I would not expect them to be detected by scientific means. People are frightened by what they cannot explain. It upsets them."

I nodded my agreement. "I learned to avoid things that upset my mother and made me feel different."

"Ah, what a shame. I went the opposite direction. I embraced what made me special and worked to develop my skills. I discovered I could learn things about people through physical contact. That is how I became aware of the song I was playing for you. I heard it in the atmosphere when I touched you the first time we met. It seemed to be haunting you." I didn't respond and he continued. "I learned that I could conjure an image and project it into the natural realm to be seen by others. That is what happened on the deck at Aeries Winery the day Sophia Russo died. Seeing her long lost love proved too much for her." He shrugged. "Finally, I discovered that, although I could not read people's minds, I could influence their minds and persuade them to cooperate with me. What you saw at the casino party was nothing. The possibilities are endless. I'll show you."

He nodded towards the open door of the great room, where Marco had appeared and a moment later, Cassandra Vaughn walked out onto the patio, with Marco trailing behind her. Her smile froze into an ugly mask when she recognized me.

"What is she doing here, Rey? You really must learn to keep better company."

Ramirez sighed and gestured to the picnic table across the patio. "Sit down, Cassandra."

She complied, watching me with undisguised distaste.

"She is still very attractive for her age, do you not agree?" he said to me.

I did not respond and he continued.

"The biggest challenge a woman faces in this world is maintaining her looks, because no matter how smart and accomplished, a woman will always be judged first and foremost on her sexual appeal. That is why beautiful women resort to desperate measures when their looks start to fade. Cassandra was once almost as stunning as Angelique is now. But her beauty is fading with age."

She looked shocked at this turn in the conversation and her face flushed with color, but she said nothing.

"She is a woman who has made her way in life by trading on her looks," Rey continued. "What would she do without them? She's not the type to try the surgery route. Her kind considers that suitable only for Hollywood actresses. But when her husband became obsessed with the legend of a ruby worn by a beautiful and powerful queen, she became obsessed, as well." He leaned towards me conspiratorially. "The ruby is rumored to hold some special powers. Perhaps she hoped one of them was the power to remain beautiful."

"Rey, where is this conversation going?" she demanded.

"Silence, woman."

His tone held none of its usual warmth or seduction and she looked stunned, but held her tongue. I glanced at Marco. He was standing behind the picnic table with an odd, blank look on his face.

"I've grown weary of this woman and her demands," Rey said to me. "It was she who first told me about the necklace. She was convinced that Vaughn had discovered a lead into its whereabouts, but he refused to discuss the subject with her. Wise man. She thought she could trade on her charms to get me to discover the truth from him and then persuade him to remember nothing except being accosted by bandits. When I explained that it would cost her more than the pleasure of her company, you will never guess what she offered, or should I say *who* she offered?"

It was my turn to be shocked. "You offered up Melanie Mayhall?" I asked her. "How could you do that to one of your own kind?" I thought for a moment. "You were the woman who lured the Sinclair girl in the parking lot last night."

"Ah, you just hit on something there, chica. Cassandra did not consider those girls her own kind. Women of a certain social class do not necessarily identify with women they consider beneath them. Her disdain was useful in certain situations, but she has outgrown her usefulness." He nodded to Marco. "Now, Marco," he said to him.

Marco reached inside his jacket and produced a gun with a silencer attached and before I could react, he shot Cassandra in the head. She slumped to the ground, dead. Then, even more shocking, without the slightest hesitation, he placed the gun against his own head and fired. He fell to the ground, not far from her. I sat there stunned, trying to make sense of what I had just witnessed.

"Do not look so surprised, Ruby. My cousin had outlived his usefulness, as well. As dedicated as he was to me, he was also secretly jealous. He did not inherit any special gifts, and he was not what you would call handsome. What he did possess was a ruthless ambition. Sometimes that quality outweighed his judgment. Cassandra was using sex to manipulate him to her advantage. He was the one who told her about our sideline with beautiful girls. And he was the one who killed David Vaughn before I could learn anything useful."

"Why?"

"He wanted to find the necklace for her, and he grew frustrated with Vaughn's refusal to talk. I am not convinced the gene completely skipped your father, as Angelique believes. His mind was very strong, and I could not penetrate it. And the Mayhall woman did not know the location of the necklace."

"And you believe the necklace really exists, and you want it that badly? Badly enough to kill people for it?"

"Why should I not believe the necklace exists? Do you not believe the ark of the covenant exists, even though it has not been seen for many centuries? The legend of the necklace has also survived for centuries and was taken very seriously by your father, a highly regarded archaeologist, which leads me to believe that he knew something. And I do not want the necklace for myself. I want it for a woman. And not just any woman. This one is special. She can have any man she wants, but I will be the man who gives her a legendary jewel." He gave me an ironic smile. "I believed I was immune to the charms of women, but she has won my heart."

"You don't have a heart. You convinced your own cousin to kill himself."

He shrugged. "Even normal people can program another person's mind into acting out a script. Government intelligence agencies do it all the time. For someone like me, it is a simpler matter, especially with a simple mind." He nodded towards Marco's lifeless form. "He had become a liability and he knew too much about my business. It will look like a murder-suicide committed by a spurned lover. Despite her concern for appearances, Cassandra was famous for her affairs. So, back to the business at hand. I want to know where to find the ruby, and you want to know where to find Angelique. Very well. Here is the deal. I had a buyer who had already paid a sizable deposit for the promise of a beautiful blonde virgin. I was to deliver her this very night. He will not be happy about the loss so, to appease him, I am substituting Angelique. She's beautiful and blonde. She's not a young virgin but, what do they say? Two out of three." He shrugged his shoulders as if he were talking about selling a car.

"Where is she now?"

"She's already gone, chica. The emissary for the buyer has already collected her. But they have not gotten far. If you tell me what your father knew about the ruby, I will tell you where to find her before they take her out of the country."

"What makes you so certain that I know where to find the ruby?"

"There were clues in your story that are not public knowledge. But, if you don't know anything more, you have nothing to bargain with, and Angelique will become collateral damage."

"Why should I believe you will let me walk away from here? Aren't I also a liability? Don't I know too much about your business now?"

"If the police are brought into the matter of the Sinclair girl, I will tell them it was Marco who was dealing in that nasty business. I will tell them I had suspicions about him, but no proof yet, and that I alerted Cassandra to that fact for her own safety, and that was why she spurned him. They will believe me. I made sure it was always Marco who communicated with the buyers, so nothing could be traced back to me. And, as you know," he smiled engagingly, "I can be very persuasive. But here is how I know that you and I will part this night and stay out of one another's way. If you try to take any action against me, I know where to find your son, the soccer player. The people I do business with do not tolerate interference, and I would only need to make a call."

He appeared to have no idea of the magnitude of his mistake. An icy resolve took root inside me.

The cards were on the table and I contemplated my options. I was still wearing my dagger, but he was sitting too close and I wouldn't be able to get it out fast enough to overpower him. I would also have trouble explaining why I had stabbed him.

"Come now, Ruby, let's be reasonable. You wanted to know what happened to your father, and I not only identified his killer, I brought him to justice for you. You don't know anything substantial about the Mayhall woman, so there is nothing to report to Jericho. And why would you? She is lost to him and he can be yours. He is what you want, no? Angelique did not tell what she saw in Cairo in hopes of winning him for herself."

He took in my look of surprise and laughed softly. "She is not your equal in virtue or abilities. Her gifts are not that impressive," he shrugged. "But I believe you are a different story. I sense real potential in you - the potential of powerful gifts at war with your sense of virtue. I don't want to kill you, Ruby. The world is more interesting with you in it."

"All right," I said. "I'm going to take you at your word, since I don't really have a choice. There was a location David shared with me on Skype. I can't tell you how to find it, but I can show it to you."

I gestured to the flames and he smiled and nodded his understanding.

"I'm intrigued," he said. "Very well. You show me what you saw, and then I'll give you Angelique's location."

I held out my hand and he went to shake it, but I held onto his hand, turned back to the flames and focused on an image of vultures circling in a twilit sky.

"Do you see the vultures flying?" I leaned into him and spoke softly into his ear without breaking visual contact with the flames.

"Yes. Well done," he returned.

"Come with me," I continued in a seductive voice. "Let's follow that trail of acacia trees and see where it leads us."

I concentrated on the flames and pulled myself into the vision, and felt the change in atmosphere – the shift in physical perception and the possibilities inherent in a different realm of existence. I stood near the remains of an ancient temple and turned to look for him.

"Are you with me?"

"Yes." He stepped out from behind a stone pillar and looked around, suitably impressed. "Are we in Yemen?"

"No. We're in Ethiopia," I smiled and pointed to an inscription on a stone wall. Above the writing was a carving of the sun and crescent moon. "This temple is believed to have been part of Sheba's empire. The writing is in the Sabaean language. My father explored the entirety of the area believed to be part of her kingdom. The necklace was reputed to be buried at the site in Marib, but he had reason to believe that was just a ploy to throw people off track, and that someone loyal to her had secretly buried it here instead. Come, I'll show you."

He smiled and followed me across the rocky terrain. "It is thrilling, is it not, to transport yourself to another part of the world by the sheer force of your will? You have been holding out, Ruby. You are even more interesting than I imagined."

He pulled me to him abruptly and stroked my face with his fingertips, then gave me that killer smile before his mouth sought mine. I fought the wave of revulsion that threatened to overtake me and willed myself to accept his kiss and smile into his handsome face, just like all the women through the ages who have had to accept unwanted advances from men as a matter of survival. Then I bid him to follow me down the trail.

"Here we are," I pointed to a stone wall in front of us with another carving of the sun and crescent moon. "This is the entrance to the abandoned mine that is believed to have been the source of Sheba's gold — an ironic hiding place for the jewel. My father said there was a clue in the inscription under the stone that points to the location of the ruby."

"What was the clue?" His tone was impatient.

"I don't know. He wasn't willing to share that part with me or anyone else at that point. He wanted to find the ruby first and get it to a safe location before he told anyone."

He stood looking at me for a moment, trying to decide whether to trust me, I imagined; then his greed got the best of him and he dropped to the ground and crawled into the opening beneath the stone. I watched from above as he pulled the matches from his pocket and lit one, carefully examining the stone in front of him for a clue.

"I'm surprised you have not come here to discover the clue for yourself," he said. "Why is that?" He looked up at me suspiciously.

"It occurred to me, but I was too afraid of what is reputed to guard this entrance."

"And what is that?"

I heard the sudden alarm in his voice. I didn't answer at first. I was distracted by the dark whisper that had called to me from the shadows ever since I entered the vision. The sound of it had become louder inside my head as we reached our destination and I wrestled with the knowledge that there might be no turning back from my actions and the moral implication they would carry. This man knew who had taken Melanie, at least initially, and where Angelique was now.

Then I remembered the way he had betrayed his own blood and the threat he made against mine, and the force of maternal instinct took over. I nodded towards the darkness behind him as the whisper inside my head entered the atmosphere around us and chanted something in an unknown language.

Ramirez turned to see. The match fell from his fingers as his scream of terror was cut short by a strike of blinding speed. He dropped to the ground and I quickly projected myself out of the vision and back onto the bench in front of the fire. The crackling flames were the only sound as I turned to find his body slumped on the bench beside me, a look of horror frozen on his face.

"A nine-foot cobra," I answered him belatedly.

I checked his neck for a pulse. There was none. It may not be possible to die in a dream, as Jewel had said, but apparently it was in a vision.

"Ruby!"

It was Derek approaching from the woods with his gun drawn, and Jack not far behind him, also brandishing a weapon. They came onto the patio, taking in the scene.

"What happened here? Are you hurt?" He holstered his weapon and took me by the shoulders as Jack checked the bodies of Cassandra and Marco.

"No, I'm fine."

"It appears that Marco shot her and then shot himself," Jack said to Derek, confusion evident in his voice.

Derek looked at me and then down at Rey's body. He reached down and felt for a pulse in his neck, just as I had.

"What happened to him?" he asked me.

"We were talking when Marco and Cassandra came out onto the patio. Marco shot her and himself, just as Jack said. And then Rey appeared to have a heart attack," I told him truthfully, as I believed that was the actual cause of his death.

"Maybe seeing Marco commit suicide was just too much for him," Jack said.

"Why would Marco commit suicide?" Derek asked.

"Rey suggested it was because he'd been spurned by Cassandra," I said.

He didn't look convinced of that as he searched my eyes. "When I couldn't find you, I knew you had managed somehow to come back here. Damn, but you're a strong-willed woman." He pulled me to him and held me for a moment.

"Derek, I was right about Angelique. Ramirez told me he sold her to compensate for the girl. He said she had already been picked up when I arrived here. And he admitted to me that he did the same with Melanie."

He looked at me, stunned, and I saw a flicker of hope light in his eyes; then he looked down at Ramirez's dead body and I saw the hope drain right back out.

"We may not be able to find either one of them now," he said, and I wasn't sure if the pain that was stabbing me was more for his despair about Melanie or the sense of guilt at war with necessity inside me.

"I'm not so sure," I told him. "I believe he was lying to me about Angelique. I think I know where to find her. Come with me."

They both followed me into the house and I led them to the den where we had rescued Meryl. I had not needed Rey to tell me where Angelique was. I had sensed it as we sat on the patio. She was not only like me, she was also related to me, and my bond with her was growing stronger. I flipped the light switch and went to the credenza where she had triggered the secret door, searching behind it for a moment until my fingers found a button. I pressed it and the bookcase swung open again. We went to the opening and there she was, tied and gagged on the same mattress that had held Meryl. She fell back onto it in relief when she saw who we were, and Derek cut her loose while I pulled off the gag.

We helped her into the den and sat her on a sofa while Jack went to get her a glass of bourbon from the bar. I recounted the bizarre events I had witnessed, sorry to have to tell her about her mother. Losing your mother is never easy, no matter what kind of relationship you had, and she looked visibly shaken as she took a drink of bourbon.

"Men were her downfall," she said. "She couldn't seem to survive without their constant admiration. My love was never enough for her and she seemed to feel the need to compete with me."

"Angelique," I cut in gently, "Rey admitted to me that he was involved in Melanie Mayhall's abduction. He seemed to think that you might have seen something in Cairo that was related to that incident. Even the smallest detail could be helpful."

Derek looked at me in surprise, then at Angelique. She looked at the floor for a moment, then up at Derek.

"I was visiting the residence of a British diplomat in Cairo with Rey. The two of them went off to have a private conversation. I wandered out onto the balcony and caught a brief glimpse of a woman being forced into the back seat of a limo. It was dark and I couldn't see very well, but she was Caucasian and she had long, dark hair. Later, when I mentioned it to Rey, he became angry. He told me it was a personal matter and warned me about sticking my nose into the affairs of powerful foreign dignitaries. I decided he was probably right, but later on I realized it was shortly after Melanie's disappearance from that area. I didn't say anything because I didn't want to give you false hope... and lose my biggest client in the process. But it could have been her, based on the glimpse I saw."

"Who was the diplomat?" Derek asked.

"A British high commissioner. I'll write down his name and address, and everyone I remember seeing there that night," she assured him.

"Well, I'm surprised the police have not arrived here yet," Jack said. "Did the Sinclair girl call them from the winery?"

"No. The police have not been alerted."

I explained how Jewel had found the girl on the parking lot and that she appeared to have had some kind of emotional breakdown and was suffering from a lack of memory of what had happened to her since she disappeared.

"That's known as a fugue state," I said. "It's fairly common in traumatic situations." I didn't mention, of course, that I believed Jewel had induced that state. "Jewel assured me she would see the girl got home safely and that perhaps it was better if she thought she had just been mugged. She also pointed out that it would be better for my career if I was not known to have been involved in this."

Angelique was watching me with an odd expression. I ignored her and focused on Derek.

"Well, she's right about that," Derek said. He looked around the room as he considered the situation. "Jack has already called in a favor to help us deal with the bodies of the guards on the trail. They probably all have criminal records, and their bodies will turn up somewhere downriver. The other three deaths are self-explanatory. Marco did commit a murder-suicide and Rey appears to have died from a heart attack."

Angelique spoke up suddenly. "I don't think it would benefit anyone for this ugly mess to go public, including my career or my mother's reputation. Her death is tainted with enough ugly circumstance." She looked at Derek. "I'm sure you can do a more effective job of investigating the lead on Melanie than the local police here, or the uninterested authorities overseas. They gave up easily enough. Why don't I just tell the police I came here for a meeting with Rey and found them all? It seems like a clear-cut case. If the Sinclair girl ever remembers anything, it will look like a bad dream or an hallucination from the drug mixed up with the account of this night from the papers."

That didn't line up with my belief that people were better off knowing the truth, but it would certainly make things simpler for everyone and I was already outnumbered on that point. I looked at Derek and he nodded his approval of the plan.

"We'll close up that secret room," Jack said, "but just to be safe, let's move that mattress out. I'm assuming it doesn't belong there?"

"No. It probably came out of the storage area downstairs," Angelique said.

Derek went to give him a hand and she told them where to take it. We closed the bookcase. Angelique wanted to see where the bodies were. She glanced briefly at her mother, but did not want to see her up close and I didn't blame her. She did, however, walk over to look at Rey. She took in the frozen expression on his face and then noticed the embers that still glowed in the fire pit.

"The storm cooled things off, but it's still rather warm out for a fire." She looked at me expectantly.

I shrugged my shoulders. "He struck me as a cold-blooded man." I said and looked her in the eye.

She glanced at Rey again and then back at me suspiciously, but she said nothing more as the men returned to the patio.

"Jack is going to stay here and help Angelique with the details while I take you back to your car," Derek told me. "And this time I'm going to make sure you do as I say." He looked down at my thigh. "Where is your gun?"

"It's in my car. I didn't want to use it. I still have my knife," I told him.

He shook his head in resignation. "You're a complicated woman."

I turned back to Angelique. "I'm sorry about your mother. Truly, I am."

I caught just a glimpse of real emotion on her face before she put on the mask of self-confidence she normally wore and nodded politely.

"You'd better put some makeup on that bruise on your jaw," I advised her, and then I headed back to the trail with Derek.

We walked along, holding hands in silence. When we reached the spot where the bodies should have been, they were nowhere to be seen, just as he had promised, and I was glad not to have to look at them again. I'd seen enough dead bodies for one night. I wondered what Derek would think if he knew how Ramirez had died.

"Derek, do you worry about the killings you've committed? I mean, for when you leave this earth. Do you believe in God and an afterlife?"

"I do believe," he nodded. "But I also believe that killing is inevitable in this world. It has been from the beginning of recorded time. I've come to terms with who I am and the role I was meant to play in this world. I can't be a watered-down version of myself, and neither can you." He pulled me to his side and wrapped his arm around my shoulder as we walked. "You've only done what was necessary and you have to just let it go."

I hoped he would always believe that. Ramirez had told me he had sold Melanie, but I didn't believe he would have ever admitted that to anyone else, or given me any details. When we arrived at my car, I asked Derek where he had put the tracer. He reached under the rear bumper and showed me the small device, before stashing it in his pants pocket.

"Don't expect me to apologize for that," he said.

I shook my head. "You're a complicated man."

I stepped into his arms and held him tightly for a moment. Then I kissed him, told him I would leave the alarm off, got into my car and drove away without looking back.

On the drive home I called Nicole to let her know what had happened and that I was okay. Jack had already assured her that Derek was helping me. Then I called Jewel. She told me that she had watched from a distance as Meryl wandered into the bar at The Loading Dock in a confused state. She appeared to be unhurt, but her purse was missing and she could not remember anything that happened after she left work the night before. The manager had called her parents to come to get her.

When I got home, I took a long, hot shower. Afterwards, I couldn't sleep, despite being physically and emotionally wrung out. I curled up in a lounge chair on the balcony outside my bedroom.

Jonah stretched out on the deck at my feet and I lay thinking about the events of the evening. My life had changed drastically and I was not certain what the future held, but I was certain of what I wanted.

Eventually, I succumbed to exhaustion and dozed off, still in the lounge chair. Sometime later I felt Derek carry me to bed. I fell into a deep sleep with his arms around me and the sound of wind chimes tinkling in the breeze.

*****

Chapter 32

It was the grand re-opening of the Paramount Theater. We had three screens, because we wanted to give the locals a more intimate, luxurious movie experience than the big cineplexes. Before the movies, though, we were hosting a private reception in the lobby, to which the local press had been invited.

Nicole was in her element. She loves an excuse to wear cocktail attire and share her work with people. I let her take the lead. I get plenty of that when I'm on a book tour.

Eventually she came over and grabbed my arm. "They want a photo of us with Jamie."

"Okay, sure."

Jamie stepped between us, all smiles, and put an arm around each of us, as photographers from several local publications snapped shots.

"How is Meryl doing?" I asked him when they stepped away.

"She's fine," he nodded. "She still doesn't remember what happened after she headed for the parking lot that evening. It appears that she was drugged but, other than that, she wasn't hurt."

"That's good. I'm glad," I told him.

"Was her purse ever found?" Nicole asked.

"It was found in some bushes across the street, where we think she might have lain unconscious and unnoticed," he told her. "Everything was there, except for her money, so it looks like it was a robbery. If they intended something more, their plans were somehow thwarted."

Nicole smiled at me when he glanced over at his daughter, talking to her mother at a cocktail table.

"We're very fortunate," he added. "Thanks for asking. And good luck with the theater. I enjoyed working with you both. I hope you'll invite me to bid on your hotel project," he grinned.

"You can bet on it," I told him, and Nicole nodded her agreement.

He gave us both a kiss on the cheek and went to rejoin his family. I imagined he would be keeping a close eye on his daughter for awhile. She might find that annoying but having a father who loves you is a precious gift.

Derek walked up with a reporter from the business journal. "They want a shot of the development team for the Stratton project," he told us and put his arms around us, just as Jamie had.

"You two get all the good-looking guys!" the female reporter teased. "Ruby, you seem to have shifted your interest from books to movies here," she said to me when the photographer was finished.

"Well, I've always been interested in movies, and restoring the Paramount has long been a dream of mine and Nicole's. We loved the history of the theater and wanted to create an upscale experience for patrons. Nicole can give you all the details."

Nicole let the reporter quiz her about both projects, while my attention was caught by Max walking through the front doors.

"Come on," I told Derek. "I want you to meet my son."

I had planned the opening night for a weekend when I knew Max had a bye in his soccer schedule. I walked into his arms and he spun me around.

"I'm so happy you could make it!" I told him. "I want you to meet someone special."

I introduced him to Derek and watched them shake hands. As far as I was concerned, that was the money shot of the evening. They launched into a conversation about economics classes, which quickly turned to sports. I suspected they were going to be good friends as Derek led him over to an appetizer stand being supervised by Jane Gordon. I stayed behind, because I had seen Angelique slip in and step back into a corner to wait for me. She was wearing a pantsuit and kept her dark sunglasses on. She was still dealing with the death of her mother and, though I had invited her, I hadn't really expected her to show up.

"I'm not staying," she said. "I just came in to say goodbye. I'm leaving for New York tonight. I had my mother's body cremated and I'm taking her ashes back for a memorial service. Then I expect I'll be getting back to business, looking for new clients."

I nodded. "It's not easy losing your mother....or your father."

I gave her a sympathetic smile, which she returned. I had told her what Ramirez had revealed to me about David's death. I'm sure it wasn't easy to learn about her mother's participation in that event, and the disappearance of women, but I believed she should know that truth.

"I thought the press coverage was reasonably low-key, considering everything," I said.

She nodded. "They were more interested in the murder-suicide angle than the apparent heart attack of a businessman they were not really familiar with. I tried to downplay the implication that my mother might have been involved with Marco and suggested instead that he had been infatuated with her and angry that he could not win her attention."

I nodded my understanding. I didn't blame her for that. She slipped off her glasses and looked at me curiously.

"The coroner told me something interesting about Rey."

"Oh?"

She nodded. "He said that he found what appeared to be the marks of a snake bite on his body, but that no trace of venom was found in his system."

"That is interesting," I said simply.

She smiled and put her glasses back on, but said nothing more. Someday, if our relationship grew deeper, I might tell her what had happened to Ramirez. I simply wasn't ready to talk about that yet.

"You take care, Angie. Feel free to call me if you'd ever like to talk. You and I have more in common than just blood, you know."

She nodded. "I'm going to go home and do some soul searching. Perhaps it's time I figured out who *I* really am."

She extended her hand and I accepted her firm shake. Then she turned and walked briskly towards the front door.

"Ms. Vaughn, can I speak with you for just a moment?" The reporter from the *Telegraph* hurried to catch up to her.

"No comment," I heard Angelique say as she went through the doors.

I wandered over to the appetizer buffet where Jane and June were fussing equally with the food and each other.

"What is that get-up you're wearing?" Jane asked as she looked her sister up and down disapprovingly. "This is a theater opening, not the Oscars ceremony."

June was dressed in a sparkly red dress, in contrast to Jane's conservative black pantsuit.

"Hey, Ruby is famous and this is her movie theater opening, so there might be some movie stars showing up." June replied. "It doesn't hurt to dress like one, so they'll be more likely to mingle with you."

"You're more likely to attract the attention of the Fashion Police," Jane told her as she turned back to the food trays. I followed the secret little smile she sent towards Jack.

Jack had escorted Nicole to the party and her parents seemed happy to see her with a date. Her father especially liked his military background and they had been sitting at a corner table, drinking and swapping stories, while Nicole met with the press.

I glanced around, feeling satisfied that the event had been a success. Max and Derek were having a beer together not far from where Jack and Lee were still talking. I realized that the one person who was missing was Jewel, but just as I was thinking that she walked through the front doors, looking lovely in a green summer cocktail dress.

"I'm so glad you could make it," I told her and gave her a quick hug.

"I wouldn't have missed it," she smiled at me.

We stepped over to a corner while the theater staff bustled around transitioning into the general public phase of the evening.

"Things are settling down in your life," she commented. "I imagine Angelique will be returning to New York now, and I'm sure it must be a relief to not have to worry about Ramirez anymore. Did you learn any valuable lessons from your encounters with him?"

"Yes," I nodded. "It's dangerous to play with fire."

She turned to search my eyes for a moment.

"Don't ever lose sight of that, Ruby. A taste of power can lead you to ruin. And don't believe everything that gets whispered in the dark."

I pushed that thought from my mind as Nicole stepped up and we started making decisions about which movie to watch.

Afterwards, Derek came home with me. Max was going out with his friends and would be sleeping over at a buddy's house. He would come home the next day to swim and barbecue with us. That worked out well because I wanted some time alone with Derek. He and Jack had been doing some research and they would be departing for Cairo on Monday to investigate the lead into Melanie's disappearance. I didn't begrudge him that. If she was still trapped in human trafficking, I hoped he would be able to set her free. If she was no longer living, I hoped he would be able to discover what had happened to her and put her memory to rest.

My girlhood dreams of giving my virginity to my husband and spending the rest of my life with him had not come true. I had been with three men in my life. The charming one I had thought was my golden prince turned out to be an unreliable, overgrown boy. The reliable one I married had crossed a line into abuse and nearly crushed my spirit, and I hadn't known how to deal with it. Over time I believe I had finally learned what to look for, and this third man seemed like the one I'd been waiting for all along. I wasn't sure what the future held for us but at least, for this night, he was mine.

*****

Chapter 33

I took my guitar and walked out to one of the boulders near the edge of the bluff beyond my pool. I hadn't played in a long time, but there's a song that has special meaning for me and I plucked it out softly and sang the lyrics. It suited my smoky alto and took me back to a simpler time. After a moment, I became aware that I wasn't alone, and turned to find Jewel making her way to a boulder behind me.

"'Fields of Gold'," I said. "It was Rachael's favorite song. They played it at her funeral."

She nodded and looked out over the river. "I wanted to let you know that I'm leaving tonight. There's something I need to take care of in Italy." She turned back to me with a smile. "You and I will meet again, but until then, I want us to stay in touch."

I had known that was inevitable, but still wasn't prepared for the rush of sadness I felt to be losing her. I set the guitar aside.

"You feel like family to me, and I'm losing you now, just like David and Sophia."

"You're not losing me, Ruby. You and I have a special connection and we will see each other again. Until then, you can reach out to me anytime you need me. And you will always carry David and Sophia with you, just like your mother and Rachael." She looked at the edge of the bluff. "Remember the married man Rachael was involved with?"

"Of course. He was a therapist she sought out for private counseling and he seduced her into an affair with him."

Jewel nodded. "Yes. I tracked him down recently. He was dying of cancer and I got him to confess his guilt to me before he died. He seemed relieved to finally tell what happened." She met my eyes. "You weren't sure how Rachael fell from that bluff. She was there with him. It was one of the places she met him regularly, away from his family and his colleagues. You hinted once that Rachael lacked a certain kind of strength, but I believe you are mistaken. Apparently, she confronted him that day and told him she wouldn't see him anymore if he wouldn't be honest about their relationship. He didn't want to let her go and they had a terrible argument. She warned him to stay away or she would tell his wife and the partners in his practice."

She looked at me steadily for a moment. "That's a lot to lose for a man with a family and a career as a therapist. A person's true character emerges in moments of desperation. He panicked and pushed her over the edge. She didn't end her own life and she was, in fact, trying to stand up for herself."

I'd suspected that possibility, but still wasn't prepared for the wave of pain that revelation brought.

"I confronted him privately to see what he could tell me," I told her, "but he swore he was in his office that evening and hadn't spoken with her. I didn't care if he did love Rachael. That didn't justify him breaking his therapeutic oath. I didn't believe anything he said, but when I questioned his receptionist, she confirmed he'd been working late that evening. I wondered if she was covering for him."

"Yes, she had been coached," she nodded. "He seduced her too, I'm afraid."

I felt suddenly deflated. Rachael had been such a good person, and she had been treated so horribly by men who were supposed to protect her.

"I wish I could see Rachael again and tell her how much she meant to me, Jewel."

"You will one day, Ruby. But you can be assured that she's happy where she is. You have your gifts and I have mine. Close your eyes."

I did and felt her light touch on the top of my head, and suddenly I was transported in my mind into a realm of light that seemed more real than anything I had ever experienced. I was floating weightless towards a balcony of white stone pillars where several people were gathered, laughing and talking. The colors were more vivid than anything I had ever seen – the physical sensations intoxicating. As I drew near the balcony, someone turned to me and I was filled with a happiness so pure it almost hurt. Rachael...

She smiled at me as the vision began to fade and I held onto it as long as I could. When I opened my eyes, I was alone on the bluff.

*****

Epilogue

I parked behind the Ruebel Hotel, where my mother had met David Vaughn, and walked stealthily to my old family property. Dusk was firmly settled in. The last of the red sun was dipping below the river's western horizon and the steady song of cicadas hummed in the trees. A light breeze chased the heavy August air down the hollow and out to the river — an early tease of autumn just around the corner.

It was deserted back there as I made my way to my mother's tiger lily patch. I crouched down and pulled a hand cultivator out of my bag. The faint light from the distant hotel parking lot was all I needed, and I struck the earth at the center point of the patch, between the two rows, and dug resolutely for several moments until I hit metal. Then I dug out around the box and drew it from the ground. It was one of those coded lock boxes you can use to store a handgun or other valuables and I tapped in the code — 0455, the time in the afternoon when Max had been born. Something only a mother would remember.

Another glance around ensured I was still alone. Just in case, my dagger was strapped to my thigh. I opened the lid, reached inside and came up with the brilliant ruby on the end of a pure gold chain. The red stone sparkled in the dying light.

Shortly before he disappeared, David had it delivered to me in a sealed package by a St. Louis attorney, who assured me he did not know the nature of the contents, along with a cryptic note from David asking me to tell no one of its whereabouts - especially Angelique. He told me he had found it in the dig in Marib, that he believed there might indeed be something unusual about it, and that he needed some time to figure everything out. He didn't tell me he was my father, but he hinted that I was special to him and promised to explain everything when he saw me in person.

I had buried it here in my mother's tiger lily patch on our old property in Grafton – a protected green space where I believed no one would find it. The subconscious connection of my real father to my mother was not lost on me. I had intended to keep it safe for him until he arrived. Except that he had gone missing and ended up dead, possibly for the necklace. If that was the case, I wanted to know who was responsible, so I incorporated some little-known facts he had shared with me about the necklace into the plot of my novel.

As all the players in the game came looking for me or the necklace, I decided to keep it where I believed it would be safer than my house, or even a safety deposit box that could be traced back to me. My father had taken it from the earth, and I had put it back in. Jonah had almost given away its location that day we visited the site with Jewel. His canine senses must have picked up my scent, even underground. I had intended to ask Sophia what she knew about the necklace that day at Aeries, but I never got the chance.

I pulled the ruby up into the light. I did have a sense that there was something special about it, but I had no idea yet what that might be. I looked closely at the setting for the stone. It had an inscription in some ancient language. That was a detail I had kept to myself. As my son had once told me, the best poker advice anyone can give you is to keep your cards close to the vest and never reveal your hand until the timing is just right.

I slipped the necklace over my head and felt the ruby settle between my breasts. For now, at least, it was a tangible reminder that I had mattered to my real father, and that was more valuable to me than a priceless gemstone. He had forfeited his life rather than lead them to me.

I carefully filled the dirt back in and patted it down. Then I brushed off the lockbox, stuck it and the cultivator into my bag and walked quickly but casually back to my car, fired the engine and drove away.

As I reached the River Road, the last of the dying sun dipped below the water's edge - a red August sun. A month of summer climax that had centered around the red fire of the ruby.

It had also introduced me to a man who touched me on such a deep level that he threatened my sense of independence; a man who was now halfway across the world chasing after the memory of another woman, while I was heading out on a quest for a white tower.

I was back at square one, with another man who was out of my reach, at least for the moment. It was like the scripture predicted – my desire was for him. The curse of Eden is alive and well. It's the price of being a woman.

*****

Upcoming Titles from Peggy Estes:

White Tower

Blue London